# Love in a Warm

# Love in a Warm Climate

## Kelley Aitken

Ingra —
for a
warm stories
cold winter!
Kelley

The Porcupine's Quill

CANADIAN CATALOGUING IN PUBLICATION DATA

Aitken, Kelley, 1954–
Love in a warm climate

ISBN 0-88984-200-0

I. Title.

PS8551.I775L68 1998    C813'.54    C98-932445-1
PR9199.3.A47L68 1998

Copyright © Kelley Aitken, 1998.

Published by The Porcupine's Quill, 68 Main Street, Erin, Ontario
NOB 1T0. Readied for the press by John Metcalf. Copy edited by
Doris Cowan. Typeset in Ehrhardt, printed on Zephyr Antique Laid,
and bound at The Porcupine's Quill Inc.

The cover, *Out of This Marsupial Night*, is after a collage (45x67 cm.,
1997) by the author. The author photo is courtesy of Billy Kung.

This is a work of fiction. Any resemblance of characters to persons,
living or dead, is purely coincidental.

Represented in Canada by the Literary Press Group.
Trade orders are available from General Distribution Services.

We acknowledge the support of the Canada Council for the Arts
for our publishing programme. The support of the Ontario Arts
Council and the Department of Canadian Heritage through the
Book and Periodical Industry Development Programme is also
gratefully acknowledged.

1  2  3  4 · 00  99  98

I wish to thank the following friends in Canada and Ecuador for their support and feedback: Brent Hayward, Moya Foley, Kathy Capello, Alick Paterson, Jim Noble, Alice Zorn, Helen Humphreys and the Women Writers Group. Loving thanks also go to my family and Frank de Jong.

For the three separate periods that I stayed in her beautiful house in the Vallé de Los Chillos, I am grateful to Annedore Muckenheim.

Special thanks go to Laurie Malabar, Elise Levine, Edna Alford, Diane Schoemperlen, John Metcalf (and his scythe).

I acknowledge, with thanks, the assistance of the Ontario Arts Council and The Banff Centre for the Arts.

For Bruce Stanley Aitken

1924–1987

# Contents

# Orchids

I AM SITTING on a huge oil pipe by the side of the dirt road high in the mountains. It's as big as a conduit but I straddle it, not really waiting for cars or trucks, although you want me to flag them down. I don't know where you are right now, high in some tree out of sight, singling out a plant from a mass of orchids draped parasitic over a branch. I don't know where you are or how long you will take or if I will be able to drag you back to the road if you fall and hurt one of your long arms or legs. The day's crisp palette surrounds me, the green and gold of vegetation at this altitude, my jeans blue and bright against the dew-shine, dark rubber of the pipe. I am exceedingly happy not just because I love you – I do, in an innocent girl-next-door way, it's all I'm allowed, it's all I allow myself – but because I am free for these few precious moments without the obligation of destination, without the expectations you have of me that I am sadly not fulfilling. It was your idea, of course; it will be years before I know enough to take these moments for myself. You've dealt this hand today; you dealt it yesterday; you are growing tired of making all the decisions, but we have not argued yet. That argument will come in a day or two in a town at a lower altitude and you will accuse and I will cry. Today your urge for orchids has lured you to strike a path through the verdant tangled growth.

You are somewhere out of sight, halfway up or down some slippery trunk and I am here and the day is perfect and I am daydreaming, I am an astronaut, I am a rider, I am a lovely lover: men flock to my side. I am writing a great book and painting many great paintings; I live on a horse ranch with a strange dark husband. I stride in and out of rooms wearing brown boots, and cream jodhpurs, my white shirt open at the neck. I am hot, exhilarated and exhausted from my day's ride; guests await me, admiring. My dogs wheel and yelp around my legs. One word from me quiets them. I am the *patrona* and my servants bring me cool drinks in tall glasses on wide, dark wood trays.

And now you are coming back, happy, the small yellow flower on its stem bouncing from the top of your knapsack. Back in the city, a week from now, it will have been transplanted, hooked into a slice of corky root and hung just outside the door to the below-ground apartment we share. By then you'll have looked it up in the orchid book and told me its name, this tiny yellow perfection, another of the small wild parasites you are determined to raise as your own.

I thought I heard a car, you say. No, a *camioneta*, going the other way. But it is still morning and though you are now all timetable and urgency, I am clinging to my roadside reverie. We left Baesa in a spitting rain, after a breakfast of instant coffee and sweet bread. Last night we met the Peace Corps woman who made us tea on a tiny spirit stove and fed us damp biscuits and told us the local cows, most of them, are sick with a parasite. She trains the farmers to use imported medicines, to sterilize the knives they wield in the simple animal surgery that is practised here. She is pretty and weary and has a thick gleaming braid of strawberry-blond hair. Prolonged loneliness has made her distrust our imported friendliness, our city chatter. She warms a bit to you because everyone does. I do not know enough botany or biology to have a real conversation with her but you and she are talking plants. She says she is always cold here, has gotten used to it. Her Spanish, like yours, is fluent.

I ask her the name of the huge white flowers we saw earlier, sagging by the dozens from trees beside the river. Angel's trumpet, she says. Oh.

Not belladonna? Close, she replies, same family. In Latin: *Solanaceae*, but you'd know it as nightshade. She pauses. And both are poisonous.

You are frowning because I've interrupted. She sees our silent exchange, the volleying of looks across this players' net we carry everywhere we go. I know that she knows the score. When we leave her to eat our dinner in the only restaurant in town I am sad in a way I don't understand.

Dinner is dinner, they say when we ask. No choice. I know they think we're silly or *tonto*, stupid. Meat. Rice. Beans. Protein for the road. I am so thirsty and the choices are the ones we will encounter everywhere: the terrible coffee or the sicksweet colas, pink and green. I whine a bit about it. You raise one eyebrow and give me that look, the one that says What do you expect?

We sleep together every night, wound around each other for warmth, because with sunset comes the bone-chilling cold. I know you resent this too at times, since mine is not the body you would choose to sleep beside or enter. This is another conversation we will have soon enough. When I ask, you will reply that you don't know how, it's been so long, women are now a foreign land. Shrugging your broad shoulders. You will say, 'I am not the man you need,' and show concern at how I've managed without it all this time. A small picture will grow in my mind of a domestic appliance, an Osterizer, dusty from disuse. Something needing service. This is how you see me.

But we have not had these conversations yet, nor even found the small brook bubbling over mossed rocks where we will wash after the descent to view the famous waterfall; nor yet shivered under each other's naked gaze, our pinkening skin rinsed clear of dust and sweat, ourselves revealed in these true mountains.

In a little over a week's time I will faint in the coastal town, overcome with heat and the effects of malaria prophylactics, and then we will board a sturdy boat that will crash into a larger ship en route to another coastal town. For a few hollow moments destiny will breathe its cool breath down our tense necks and the world will stop and then we, with all the rest, the too-many passengers on this boat without lifebuoys or rafts, will move, *en masse*, a giant beetle with many legs and arms, stretching, reaching, leaping, flowing in mid-ocean from one boat to the tanker that is heading back in the direction from which we came until, only-in-Ecuador, the group takes up a collection to bribe the new *capitan* to change course. We will get where we are going one half day late, the last to leave the tanker because we are gringos and neither understand the etiquette nor have the confidence to jump queue into the small overloaded *canoas* ferrying passengers to shore for two hundred *sucres* a head. News of us will have reached the town where we are expected, news that *los rubios*, the blonds, were on the boat that broke and will be coming. When? *Ya mismo*, meaning: now, soon, someday, maybe, I don't know.

All of that is still to come, as is the hot town at the edge of the jungle with cockroaches larger than I could have imagined and a shit-smeared toilet too far down the hall and open-sided buses and ragged running children, pointing, laughing, with whom I play a kind of waving game that infuriates you, and why is that? Because they stare more openly at me? We will buy green metallic bugs and black velvety butterflies with neon markings in the one real tourist town we hit during this five-day circling tour of ours, the butterflies folded shut and labelled in tiny triangles of waxed paper, the bugs rolled in toilet paper and nailed into a balsa box.

The owners of the store will serve us something sweet and steeped and alcoholic and show us how to inject water from a syringe into the dried thorax of the butterfly to force it open for display, and they will take us to the hot springs, these people who adopt us, these people you always, always charm.

And still to come is a trip upriver by canoe to the house on stilts where the beautiful American artist lives with her trail-guide husband and their wild child son who pees like a dog because he has no human playmates, only this old and faithful German shepherd. While you are talking trails and botany with her Ecaudorian husband, she will show me pictures of her paintings, Bosch-like and disturbing, insisting that I read each title, discuss and respond to each image so that we will be tired and ready for bed before any mention is made of the fact that I too am a printmaker and painter. I am being con-quered skilfully by this belladonna, she is a pale heavy fruit hanging from a dark tree at the border of my dream when I finally fall asleep after taking fright at the tarantulas in the outhouse. The next morning she will conquer you but it will be more mutual, her beauty firing hot and white against yours, and you will talk about orchids as if nothing else existed in the world. I will be ignored but not mind it too much, stunned by the dawn beauty of the jungle, the morning glories big as saucers, beaming a blue so electric it hurts my heart. Her husband has found orchids no one has docu-mented before. Somehow she makes it sound as if this, too, is her accomplishment. When we leave their home, travelling again by canoe, I will not be sad to say goodbye, although I'll feel diminished and frumpy. Even you will look paler, bleached by her white-hot need.

But none of this has come to pass because you are still out of sight, shimmying up or down some wet tree. And I cannot beckon that part of me to leave that roadside, to come down off that wide round oil pipe. I cannot take her into a future which is now my past, she will not budge or remove herself from reverie, from dreaming. She is whistling softly and smiling at the weeping gold and green surrounds, she is in gestation, waiting for a sign, a symbol, an orchid disentangled from its sybaritic perch, an orchid bouncing in its new found and temporary nest and everything she wants and needs, she has not learned yet. Because it's an art. Wanting. Needing. Knowing who you are.

It's only now, down the long tunnel of memory, that I see her innocence, perched and taking nourishment from air. You will be a part of a campaign, organized, it seems, to take that from her and so it is with the obstinacy of a child, with the grip of an orchid on its borrowed branch, that she is clinging to the time before the pain.

# The Shark

———

*Contrary to popular belief, the vast majority of encounters between man and shark end badly for the shark.*

JANE IS SNORKELLING, floating in the cool shadow of Cigar Rock, off the island of Bartolomé. She counts at least five *loros* in the immediate vicinity. That's the Spanish word for both the parrot and the brilliantly coloured fish beneath her, drifting sideways on the current. From a hole in the reef comes a tiny swimming sun, radiantly yellow. And here's a king angelfish, outlined in electric blue, flicking his tail. He's luminescent. Even the velvety black of his body seems to glow, even the white patch behind his gills.

There's a gender bias to all this lavish colour, Jane thinks. But the males have their job to do, luring potential predators away from the egg-laying females. Luring, lurid – she's never before realized how those words are connected. The azure parrotfish is a radioactive turquoise. And the rainbow wrasse, in the stage they call 'supermale', is almost too small for the colours lavished on it. Yellow, magenta, indigo.

Over the throaty repetitions of her own breath, she hears buzzes and clicks, something wave-like and swooshing – the tide? – and a long zing, like crickets in summer.

At the edge of her vision, a sheet of rubber pauses. Pulses.

'Spotted eagle ray.' She's said it aloud, the words burbling around the snorkel's mouthpiece, echoing in the trapped air of her mask. The sensation, more guttural and physical than talking on land, makes her chuckle. Well, that's a pleasant change. How long has it been since she laughed? Ten months? A year?

A school of striped snapper flows around the outcroppings

of coral, hundreds moving as one, skirting the plump anemones. She reaches a languid hand into their midst – now a parted curtain, two halves flashing a silvery semaphore: Goodbye, goodbye.

A tiny black torpedo caroms through the corner of her vision, the Galapagos penguin, dapper as a butler. Follow me, he says, but Jane cannot. The guides have assured her that sharks in these waters are well fed. But what about the scars and scrapes in the bronze hides of sea lions? What about the ones that didn't get away?

Sharks, like wolves, cull the weak from the herd. She thinks they'd smell it on her, the thing that sets her apart from all the other people on the boat.

A cruise ship in the Galapagos. The tourists have come for pleasure and eco-education. The crew like it because it's a better job than most. Jane is here because she's desperate, although she doesn't think it shows. She wants to shake off the grey thing that has built itself around her since her father's death. You must have been close, say the few people she tells about her father.

'Sort of,' she replies.

'But you loved him,' they say.

Love. It is the word used to cover all that.

———

*A shark is always 'listening', because its sensory organs are always on. It is able to pick up the slightest disturbances in the water, and it is especially sensitive to the sounds made by, or reminiscent of, a wounded fish.*

Jane and her father are speeding across the bay under a leaden sky. It rained last night. The boat needs to be drained of the several inches of water that sloshed around their feet when they got into it, moments ago. With the bow up, the collected rainwater has formed a small, slanted lake in the stern. He has already told her – gruffly, as is his manner – what they're going to do. He has not asked if she understands his instructions. Jane, aged ten, knows that she has been selected for this task only because her brother, two years younger, is away overnight at someone else's cottage. Her father shouts something above the roar of the motor, motions Jane over, lifts her into the driver's seat. He moves to the back of the boat to pull the plug. Jane, rigid with fear, is driving but not driving, arms at right angles to her body, a stick person, a doll, robotic at the helm. She stares straight ahead, gripping the wheel, feels the projection of the boat as a steel arrow, aiming. True. On this trajectory they cross into an adjunct bay, are now on a direct path towards its dark shore.

Turn the wheel, a voice is saying, inside Jane's head. To starboard. Since they arrived at the rented cottage on Lake Muskoka, her father has been addressing them, both his kids and his wife, in the language of the navy. He is impatient when the children move to the wrong side of the boat, or stand on the dock, wide-eyed with incomprehension. Jane knows port, now, and starboard, knows bow and stern and half-hitch and halyard. But just the words. Can't make her body translate meaning into movement: turn, steer, bend; her hands gripping the white wheel are locked into rigidity and in her mind a terrified voice is screaming, Daddy, daddy, daddy, we're going to crash.

Jane is staring at the shore, pleading with it to remain where it is, not to be rushing towards them, an inevitable wall of tree and rock. Screaming silently for her father to come forward. Maybe she finally murmurs, Dad, and then a little louder, Dad, and maybe she also says, I can't turn. Years later she's not sure if she said anything at all, but somehow he is suddenly at her side and almost on top of her, shoving her sideways in the seat, yanking the wheel roughly. And so simply, they are moving out of the confines of the smaller bay and towards the open water of the lake. Relief floods Jane; she thinks she might cry. Her father says nothing and returns to the stern. In the time he takes to reinsert the plug, Jane invents and lives another life with him: they have driven without hesitation into the woods, have sheered off the surface of the lake into the cool green shade, and they are going on like that forever, she and her dad, all by themselves in the wet, white boat.

———————

*It is unlikely that any animal is really unpredictable, for the concept of random or haphazard behaviour would be inconsistent with most natural laws and the behaviour of most animals. We are calling our own inability to understand the action of sharks their unpredictability, while the very success of the sharks should tell us that they react regularly (for the shark, at least), in a variety of ways, to a variety of stimuli.*

There are black fields of lava, ropy *pahoehoe* and brittle *ah-ah*. On an island covered with the purplish-red of portulaca, Jane sees her first land iguanas, and falls in love with these benign miniature dinosaurs. Their diet consists of prickly pears and cactus blossoms, large blooms that appear incongruously at the periphery of its pads. Into the homely, happy faces, into that wide, frowzy grin, the yellow petals fold and crumple and disappear.

Here in the Galapagos, a place he never visited, Jane thinks of her father. The portulaca recalls one of his projects, a rock garden in the backyard of their suburban home. Once a week, she can speed in a small white boat to the pier at South Plaza, she can set foot on the rock and sand beach and look over the island, and she is soothed a little by the sight of the humble plant blanketing its gentle slope.

---

*It is when they open their mouths to bite that the teeth of sharks become visible, because most sharks have the ability to protrude their jaws, thus erecting the teeth to bring them into play. As the upper jaw protrudes, the snout is flexed upward to get it out of the way, and without having to roll over at all, a shark can bite a large object head-on.*

Partway through a fine arts degree at York, she is still living at home. Entering the basement workshop, her father's sanctuary, she addresses his back.

'Dad?' No reply. Selective deafness, she knows she does it too. In the big family, they've all found ways to shut each other out.

'Dad?' She waits, staring at his back for what seems an interminable period. 'James!' she barks. He turns and cocks an eyebrow at her. There are beads of sweat on his forehead and wood chips in his hair. A pencil salutes her from the top of his ear. She wishes he would smile.

'I want to make Rick a paintbox,' she says. 'For Christmas,' she adds lamely. She's not sure her father likes this new boyfriend. He didn't like the former one. About Rick, who is also an art student, he has only asked, 'And how does he expect to support himself?'

A fair question, she supposes, considering his own experience. He'd shown talent as a kid. When it came time for college, he'd enrolled – enthusiastically – in architecture. After one year, a professor took him aside, 'You'll never be more than a mediocre technician. Find another field.'

'Best advice I ever had,' he says. And then, about his decision to go into sales, 'Smartest thing I ever did.'

She alternates between wanting to give it back to him – art – and wondering if he's waiting for her to get the hint.

[ 19 ]

Smarten up. Settle down.

He turns to the thing he was working on when she came in. Dad, she wants to scream, listen to me. It takes her a full minute to realize he is, in fact, tidying a space for her at the workbench.

'Like this?' he asks, making deft marks on wood with the pencil he's pulled from behind his ear.

'Unh, sure.' The idea of the box bangs against her brain, like a moth on a screen, trying to get through, to get out. Shouldn't we discuss it, she wonders?

He's making more marks along the plank, flicking the switch on the saw, pulling plastic goggles off a shelf above his head on the cement wall. She takes a step forward, reaches out her hand for the goggles; her heart rises and lodges in her throat.

But he's doing it for her, cutting the plank into five pieces: a base, two rectangular sides, and ends shaped like the houses in a child's drawing – his design. There are scraps left over when he's done. He tosses them into a plastic bin that bristles with odd-shaped and pointed pieces of wood. The saw whines into silence when he flicks the switch off, pushing the goggles up on the top of his head. She can hear his breath now, a regular but also ratchety sound, though he hasn't smoked in years. In each of the ends, he drills holes for the dowelling that will serve as a handle. When he's finished he pushes the pile of wood over to where Jane is standing. He tosses the goggles onto the shelf.

'Clean up when you're done,' he says, walking out through the furnace room. She stares after him, feels the familiar guilt and yearning.

Now she hears heavy footsteps overhead, in the kitchen. A cupboard door pops closed. A few moments later, the thunk of the fridge door. She cannot hear the rest, but knows the routine, has done it so often herself it's almost a ritual.

The perfect martini. She's been making them since she was about eight, thrilled to have the errand, the responsibility. Ice tinkling in the glass and the occasional hiss when the vermouth bottle was opened. He'd been glad to demonstrate, years ago. 'Just a drop,' he'd said, 'a *soupçon*,' using the word with pleasure. And Jane, later – years later, both before and after his death – recognized the unconscious and unstated desires in her father's penchant for French words and cuisine, for the Italian leather shoes he bought himself and the shimmering silver stockings he gave their mother one Christmas. He wanted another life, something more cosmopolitan and less predictable than the six kids and a sprawling house in the suburbs, golf on the weekends, a gin-induced nap in front of the TV every single night, the look of judgement on his wife's face, and now his kids' too. Their family has congealed around this: he's the bad guy, the problem. If she only knew what to do, how to fix it. Fix him.

'The perfect martini,' he said cheerfully, rummaging in the depths of the refrigerator, 'starts with peel.' He emerged from his search, triumphant, lemon held aloft. With a flourish of the Henckel paring knife – there were others in the drawer, but this was the one he chose, every time – he removed a small strip of the yellow skin, an inch long and a third as wide, lined with the barest layer of pith. He wiped this around the perimeter of the glass before dropping it in. The peel was anchored with ice; eight or ten cubes for the stout old-fashioned glass. Over this he poured Beefeater's gin, clear and faintly bluish. Finally, the requisite dribble of vermouth. Sometimes the peel slid up between the ice, floated around on the surface of the drink. Gripping the wide glass in a broad hand he'd plunge his index finger into the icy liquid to push the yellow strip under again.

---

*A shark has no bones. The skull, spinal column and some fin supports are all cartilaginous, and since there is no rib cage or other supporting structure, the shark is held together, as it were, by its muscle and skin.*

The tantrums if he knocks over a glass. More as he gets older. His face turning red, daughters rushing to get a cloth. He's never hit them. But the air around him smells violent, like something about to explode.

———

*Sharks are denser than water and must develop a certain amount of dynamic lift to avoid sinking. Most sharks solve the problem by constantly swimming.*

Off the port or starboard, when the sun has passed beneath the horizon and the ship's lights illuminate a small, circular patch of sea, Jane sometimes sees a school of golden rays, like underwater kites or dozens of undulating hankies. And every night after she crawls into her berth, she is rocked to sleep by the lilt and lift of the boat's hull on the gentle swell. 'Sleeping on the back of the whale,' she writes, in letters home.

———

*Sharks are attracted by the struggles of a hooked fish, and many an angler has seen his catch destroyed by a shark that has beaten the man to the gaff.*

It's a rare treat, being taken to dinner by her father; she's not sure how it came about. A reward, she wonders, for splitting up with 'that artist fellow?' The restaurant is a Spanish one Jane has wanted to try for some time, but even before crossing its threshold, she feels tense. What will they talk about?

It's early yet, the restaurant is less than half full, but Jane is sure that all the other patrons are aware of their entrance. How could they not be when he's ordering a double martini in a booming voice as he strides through the elegant room. 'Very dry, maestro,' he says, 'with a twist.' And Jane is saying, 'Dad, shhhh,' but her words are whispered, an ineffectual counterpoint to the main melody, her father's happy baritone. 'And I mean drrryyy. You can just pass the cork over the top of the glass.'

'And for the young lady?'

'White wine,' Jane murmurs. 'Just a glass.'

At a nearby table are two couples, grey-haired. One of the women leans across the table and whispers something to her friend. The other woman's eyebrows disappear under the starched bangs of her expensive hair. Is it her husband who twists around in his seat, casts an appraising look at Jane as she lowers herself awkwardly into the chair the maître d' is holding. Jane flushes and drops her eyes, but not until she's caught the subtle wink. Oh, God, is that what they think? Under-aged mistress. Sugar daddy.

For just a moment her thoughts stray there.

DON'T YOU DARE! It's a braying fog-horn, assaultive. Has she actually said it? Out loud? She grinds her teeth together and sneaks a look at the Nosy Parkers. No. They aren't even looking now. And the sigh she releases is followed by a little brain flutter, toward and again away from the verboten.

She stares hard at the menu in her lap. The words swim a bit, scrabbling ants on the heavy cream paper. They sort themselves into single Spanish phrases followed by descriptive paragraphs in English. Italic. No prices. '*Paella*,' she says. And yes, that was out loud, a little mouse-squeak of a word, but her pronunciation is good, the double *l* elastic, like a *y*. Even though she's dying of embarrassment, she's enough of a snob herself to manage that.

Now the maître d' has left and her father is chatting with

the waiter, announcing that they speak a bit of 'the lingo'. Whereupon he beams expectantly at Jane.

'I don't really know any Spanish, Dad,' Jane says, trying not to look at either of them.

'*Como esta usted?*' queries her father, stretching the verb so that it comes out sounding like estowwa. He is smiling broadly.

'*Bien gracias, señor, y usted?*' replies the waiter. He has dealt with this kind of exchange before.

'*O sole mio,*' her father says, with a theatrical gesture Jane has seen a million times, his wrist describing a circle while his arm waves away from his body.

'Daddy,' Jane grimaces, shocked to find herself speaking to him in the childish form of address, 'that's Italian. Can we just order?'

―――――――

*Though they are silent themselves, sharks are very much involved with sound, since it has now been shown to be their most effective long-range sense. However, it is not altogether clear how a shark perceives sounds, with what, or if they distinguish between sound as we know it and very low-frequency vibrations.*

On the boat when she talks to the tourists or the crew, she's aware of the grey room, its walls defining a cool space around her. When someone makes a special effort, she responds, until inside her head she hears a door snick shut.

But on the islands, Fernandina, Floreana, Santiago, she wanders away from the tour groups, bare feet on hot pumice, T-shirt tied and tucked above her midriff. She lies down on sand or grey-black lava and closes her eyes to the bleaching sun, the scent of baking skin in her nostrils. Sally Lightfoot crabs emerge from solid whorls in the dark looping rock. They see her and scuttle back to shelter. Sometimes tears squeeze out between her closed eyelids. The weight on her chest lifts a little, just a little.

———————

*Approximately 70 percent of (the shark's brain is) devoted to the olfactory function (which accounts for) the references to the shark as a 'swimming nose'.*

Her father is in a downtown hospital, following the second of the hip replacements. Jane walks into the semi-private room and over to her father's bed. His eyes are closed. She touches his hand.

'Dad?'

His eyes open wide. In an uncharacteristic gesture, he reaches for her hand and presses it his lips, 'Thanks for coming, Janie.' He hasn't called her that since she was a kid. She blinks back sudden tears, and busies herself with removing her jacket.

He's dying.

Neither of them can acknowledge this yet. He says, 'Something in my blood – they're doing tests,' The persistent jaundice stains the skin of his withered cheeks. She empties his urine bottle for him, alarmed by the liquid that pours into the toilet, dark as strong tea.

Risks the rage.

'Have the doctors said anything about liquor?'

The silence around him implodes. Stay back, it says. Stay behind that line.

———————

*Sharks have been known to feed when they're full, and starve to death when they should be hungry. Some sharks migrate thousands of miles, while others seem to stay in one place all their lives.*

Her skin is bronzing. She's gaining weight on the ship's rich cuisine, filling out like a Latina. She walks the outer decks, trailing a hand along sun-warmed wood and metal railings. The crew are a cocky bunch, their flattery of her routine, an automatic response to her blond hair and slim legs. She ignores all but the third engineer, in whose company she almost relaxes. He wants, he says, to learn English. His shy efforts at seduction comfort her even as she recognizes their inevitable failure. Trapped in the celibacy of grief, Jane fears the end of his attentions but cannot reach out to make him stay.

---

*A shark's head is covered with a series of sensory pores called the ampullae of Lorenzini ... it is now accepted that (these) are electroreceptors. As an electrosensitive animal, a shark can also detect large-scale electric fields, such as the magnetic fields of the earth and the changing polarity of moving water.*

When the news is delivered to her parents in another hospital, her father makes one request of his wife.

'Don't tell the kids.'

He means their children, now in their twenties and thirties. Because he's dying, because she herself feels guilty – in the last twenty years she has been more mother than wife – she grants him this last wish.

Yet, in the hospital for that first visit, Jane knows at a cellular level that she is losing her father. The whole time she is at his bedside or wheeling him through the halls in a squeaky blue wheelchair, she will be in a subtle panic to frame herself as the daughter he wants, a young woman on the road to financial security and success. She will sense the need to do this, without knowing why; she will feel scared and want to cry. She will pause at the elevators after each short visit, feeling a pull to return to his room, throw herself across his chest and burst into childish tears. Each time, she will resist the impulse; she will carry the lump of what she knows already, and yet cannot know, out into the city's noisy streets.

———

*Almost any large carnivore will eat human remains that it encounters in its own environment...*

The land and sea are beautiful, an almost-balance for the grey weight she carries, but the job feels demeaning, silly. She's running the ship's boutique. There is just room enough for her to stand in the tiny shop, among stacks of T-shirts in plastic bags, boxes of toiletries and sun-visors emblazoned with the ship's name. She sells through a window space, leaning forward on a glass-covered shelf, postcards of frigate birds and yawning sea lions beneath her elbows. Four times a day she removes the board that covers the window to sell to the tourists, sunblock for their noses, film for their cameras; stumbling over the Spanish words, smiling wider than an iguana when she can't express herself in the language of her employers and clients.

———

*Vision in water is a different problem altogether, since one of the notable properties of water is its density. Light does not pass through water nearly as readily as it passes through air, and in order to function efficiently, an animal that lives in water must rely on other senses in addition to sight. Sharks' eyes are well designed for the function they have to perform, that is, finding prey after their longer-range senses have enabled them to locate it from beyond the range of their vision.*

When the call comes from the hospital, one of her sisters

crying into the phone, 'Dad's dead,' Jane gets out of the double bed she has been sharing with her mother because they've all stayed overnight – the bed her mother has jumped out of to answer the phone – and walks straight into a grey room.

At first no one notices. Everyone is busy with feelings of their own, with their own confusions. A death in the family. No one is really prepared. They stare blankly at one another; the ties that normally bind them, one to the other, gone suddenly slack.

Or maybe everyone is in a grey room, like Jane. She hasn't described it to herself as a room yet, she just thinks this is what happens to you when someone dies. She goes to the hospital to see her father's body and the grey comes with her. It laps at the edge of her vision, envelops the body on the bed; the old face with its open mouth and shut eyes; then the room, the window looking out over a parking lot, a highway.

A watch on the wrist of the dead body beeps, shrill in the still of the room; two quick stabs of sound, deep red in colour, piercing the grey. Jane laughs, surprised, horrified, and immediately feels foolish.

———

*All sharks have teeth. Teeth are the very essence of the shark, without them it would be just another fish in the eyes and imaginations of the world.*

They've walked inland on Genovesa, skirting the iguana nests, small pits dug out of the sand. They've seen lizards and mockingbirds, frigates and finches, and all three species of boobies. The island is famous for the smallest of these, the red-footed, which nest in trees. Some of the birds patently ignore the bending heads and pointing cameras of the tourists; they turn their backs, or tuck a long blue beak under one wing to sleep. But others return the stares of their visitors, as curious about humans as the humans are about them. Jane is struck by the equanimity of the creatures of these islands, so accepting of the repetitive invasions, the constant observation.

At the end of the hike the group returns to the beach. Jane is first into the water. She spits into her mask, rubs the glass and then pulls it over her face, tightening the rubber straps and biting down on the rubber mouthpiece. Behind her, members of the group strip off shorts, shirts, hats and sandals. Their chatter and laughter is cut short when she bends and swims.

Just like that, she is alone with only her own breath, magnified, and the push-pull of the current. The water is murky, the sand of this cove so fine it is stirred up by the repetitive wash of the tide. The snorkelling won't be great. Still, she swims toward the eastern arm of the cove, enjoying the instant solitude, the invigorating hug of the sea.

She has been in the water for about ten minutes, moving forward slowly, when she sees a large dark form in the cloudy water. Boulders, three in all, are spread out over the white sand floor. She swims towards the largest, attracted by something extending from its base. At this angle it looks like an old-fashioned sled, the parallel runners shoved up underneath the massive rock.

Part of a shipwreck, Jane thinks.

The water is no less particulate here than it was near the beach. She is about a metre distant and ready to place a foot on the nearer of the two shapes when she realizes that the forms beneath her, while sleek, are not metal or wood at all. She retracts her foot and pushes with her arms at the water in front of her chest. She swallows the scream that wants to erupt out of her nose and mouth because of what she was about to do – touch the closer of two basking sharks. Afraid to turn her back on them, she continues to swim backwards, awkwardly, an aquatic quadruped in retreat. There is a thumping sound. Good God. It takes her a few seconds to realize that it is her own heart. If she weren't so scared, she'd laugh. Hours later she will, telling the story. '*Bom bom bom bom bom,*' she'll say, 'Just like the soundtrack from *Jaws*.'

For now though, she is intent on covering distance quickly, and on her silent prayer. Don't wake up. Don't wake up.

―――――

*Feeding frenzies, or 'mob feedings' do occur, but they do not take place frequently, and there is some question whether they happen in nature, or if they are completely man-inspired, and therefore atypical behaviour.*

They'd never said it while he was alive. That one word. 'Alcoholic.' Now it's a released bird, it beats its wings noisily through every conversation. Jane marvels at the ease with which her siblings use it, as if it explained everything. It's like they're already wiping the slate clean, starting fresh. When she says it, it has the feel of a pebble in her mouth, it tastes of dust.

Jane goes to the funeral parlour with her sister Beth. Beth is the one who called, crying, from the hospital. Beth's grief is dramatic, generous, she is sharing it with her friends on the phone daily. Beth and Jane volunteer to pick out the urn, because their mother is not used to making decisions. She wept with relief when they offered.

The funeral director is wearing formal dress, grey striped pants and a cutaway jacket. He leads them up a wide stairway to his office. Once inside he beckons them to take two leather armchairs in front of a dark wood desk. The lights have been dimmed. His expression, something between a sad smile and a bemused frown, remains unchanged for the duration of their thirty-minute visit. Jane wonders if his face is locked into this shape, if it's what he offers his wife from their shared pillows, and shows to the bank teller, the gas station attendant, the pharmacist.

She wants to say, 'Wipe that stupid look off your face!' She'd like to do it for him. The thought is accompanied by a telltale contraction in her gut and tingling up and down her spine. Where she clutches the arms of her chair, the wood is now slick with sweat.

It's been off and on like this for two days. Savage growls rising from her belly and lodging in her throat – because of course she's stifled them. As difficult to suppress is the electricity singing through her limbs, yearning to lash out, to make bruising contact with flesh. Friends, family, even strangers on the street. The urge is undiscriminating; everyone's a potential target.

Surrounded by the tastefully appointed furnishings, staring at the tastefully arranged face, she plots where the punch would land.

'Smack-dab in the kisser,' she mutters.

Her sister and the undertaker look up quickly. 'Excuse me?' he says. Beth gives Jane a sharp look. Though younger by four years, she has an air of authority. Jane is grateful for it now.

'Nothing,' she replies.

I'm losing my mind, she thinks. The voice inside her head is getting louder, a mutinous litany, 'Crazy, crazy, crazy,' it is saying. She's squirming in her chair now, uncomfortable. The undertaker continues in a modulated voice. Beth's finger traces a line down the paper he has placed in front of the sisters.

Jane has locked her arms around her chest, an impromptu straitjacket. The voice is heckling, hysterical. She's terrified she won't be able to keep it in.

'Crazy, crazy,' it says.

Oh, God, she thinks. Help me.

And just in time, the grey moves in on her; it muffles the voice. Inside the grey room, Jane is prevented from exploding. The urns are in a glass cabinet. She and Beth pick one. Simple and brass, it is square and costs far too much.

---

*Sharks have achieved the most advantageous position in the ocean – they are the apex predators, and have been so for millions of years. This is surely one definition of success, although empirically it does not guarantee survival – think of the carnivorous dinosaurs.*

They travel between the large and small islands of the archipelago in a circuit that repeats itself every seven days. From the guides, Jane has learned that the whole of the Galapagos, its lands and offshore waters, are protected by international law. The tourists are admonished against removing even the smallest shell or stone from its beaches. For some reason, this makes her feel safe, as if she too were protected.

It is a month since they left the Ecuadorian mainland. The crew are restless. There is plenty of food in the ship's kitchens but they pester the captain to let them fish. And although it is illegal, the ship is well out of sight of other craft. He finally okays the hanging of a line over the stern. The men's spirits are much improved, focused. Between their chores they look down over the ship's railing and squint to see beneath the water's sparkling surface.

---

*Like other predators, sharks eat enough to maintain their biological equilibrium and also like other predators, they don't spend any more energy than they have to in the process.*

She can't cry. Instead she alternates between manic anxiety and a kind of numbness. 'Fuzzy' she says, trying to explain it to her boyfriend, 'a stupid feeling, really.' She's been talking for about twenty minutes, hoping for a sympathetic response. It's 'what passes,' she supposes, 'for rest in a body that isn't getting any.'

But sleep is not Doug's problem. He manages eight, ten hours a night. She doesn't tell him she's more jealous of that than if he'd taken up with another woman.

'I dunno, my cells feel hypersensitive, and my neck feels like there's a steel rod shoved through it and my teeth feel, well, this is going to sound really strange Doug, they feel sharp and cold all the time. You don't think I'm sick, do you, coming down with something? Doug?' But he isn't listening. It's been like this for a while. When he's over, he mostly just watches her small black-and-white television.

He's starting to balk at her need, the clinginess. They'd only been going out for a few months when her dad died. He's younger than she is. He's already said, 'You should be over this now.'

Over what? she thinks. What is he talking about?

She uses every kind of emotional blackmail to get him to her apartment on weeknights as well as the usual 'date' evenings. And sex, though she doesn't really want it, sometimes keeps him from going home.

Her libido isn't dead so much as AWOL, on vacation. His tongue in her mouth reminds her of frogs, no, more like liver. Making love seems like a lot of weary bumping. She wishes it would put her to sleep the way it does him, but she lies beside him on the futon, smelling their combined scents, plucking at stray hairs on the rumpled sheets. She gets up and goes to the bathroom one night, returning with a glass of water. It isn't planned so much as just a natural flow of events. He's snoring. She throws the water at his face.

'I don't know who you are any more!' he yells twenty minutes later, damp curls of hair bouncing on his forehead as he bangs out the door with his duffel bag.

He won't be coming back. The long slow torture of her own company in the following months gradually turns into total insomnia. It's a fall day when Jane finds herself staring into a shop near her apartment. She studies her face, its vague reflection in the window. Her skin is pale and there are dark shadows under her eyes. She focuses on what's behind the glass, sunny scenes depicted on glossy posters, the mock beach that has been set up on the inside sill, complete with coconuts, a plastic pail and shovel. She's passed this every day for as long as she's lived in the neighbourhood. But today she sees it for the first time. A travel agency.

Escape. The idea appeals in a way that nothing has in ages.

There's genuine relief on her friends' faces when she tells them. 'Just what you need,' says one.

'You haven't been yourself,' says another.

A third friend, an older woman, offers the name of someone who hires crew for cruise ships. Jane makes a call. She is surprised at how easily the plan unfolds. In a few weeks it's all arranged; a trip to the equator and a shipboard job while touring the tiny islands of Darwin's archipelago.

---

*It has often been observed that sharks take a long time to die.*

The third engineer appears, breathless, at the boutique's window where Jane is stacking T-shirts. *'Una pelicula,'* he demands, a film for his camera; he wants to photograph the shark.

'What shark?' Jane asks.

*'Un tiburon enorme,'* he says by way of explanation, as he hurriedly loads his camera, tossing the empty film box aside

and racing off towards the metal stairs between decks. Half an hour later Jane closes up the shop and goes to see for herself.

She walks toward the crowd on the lower deck. At least a third of the tourists are here and many of the crew. A camera flashes. Jane mutters, *'Permiso, permiso,'* and two or three people move aside to allow her an unobstructed view.

She stares in shock, hardly breathing for several minutes. The shark is huge. A thick rope wrapped around the tail and over one of the metal rafters holds most of the long body aloft, with only the snout and jaws pressing against the floor. At its neck the flesh has rolled, plump wrinkles that remind Jane of a child's tummy. A blood slick has spread outward in a circle. One of the crew mops at the edge of the dark red, constantly replenished puddle.

Jane feels an answering tug of gravity, of blood draining from her brain, and the shimmery aura that tells her she's about to faint. She's experiencing tunnel vision; the crowd has disappeared and only the shark, grey and totemic, remains in focus.

She should sit down; she should put her head between her knees.

But now, instead of losing consciousness, there is another sensation, like a cramp but without pain, as if her lungs, dia-phragm and stomach were realigning themselves.

Something is happening to the shark. Jane senses as much as sees movement in the air immediately surrounding it. For the first time she realizes that the shark isn't really grey after all, but almost glowing, lit-from-within, that quality peculiar to creatures of the sea.

In her chest and belly, something pulls. The tears spill over her lashes.

So maybe it's an optical trick. Or the yearning of her own spirit, shut down so long. Whatever the source or the reason, she sees an aqueous light flowing from the shark, travelling up the rope, along the rafter, out through the wide opening at the side of the ship.

Ashes to ashes, they say, and what is from the sea, taken back to the sea. After the tourists are in bed tonight, the shark will be cut down, cut up and carted away in plastic tubs. The metal flooring will be hosed clean, blood and intestines sluiced over the side as small fish and large rise with open mouths, and night-hunting gulls snap bits of gut off the water's surface.

In the kitchen the chef and two men will work side by side, slicing most of the shark meat into steaks and freezing those in plastic bags for the crew. A small portion of the meat will be cubed and marinated in the juice of several lemons, a surprise on the lunch menu: *Cebiche de tiburon*.

But that is tomorrow. Here, now, the grey room folds in on itself and disappears. Drifting through the evening air, ephemeral as a trail of phosphorescence on an opaque sea, lifting silvery and sheer toward the stars' embrace, is – Jane is certain of this – the spirit of the shark.

And her grief rises with it, letting go.

---

The italicized portions of 'The Shark' are from Richard Ellis, *The Book of Sharks*, Grosset & Dunlap, New York, circa 1976.

# The River

IT IS A CHILD, in the end, that releases Gaby from the thick cocoon of her grief: Ana's daughter visiting for an afternoon; Ana preparing an *encocada* and baking *pan*, for the first time too preoccupied to tend to Gaby's needs. She bends frequently to hug one of her three grandchildren or tousle their hair, digging in the pocket of her apron for wrinkled *sucres* so that Juancito, the eldest, can buy *caramelos*. The boy runs out the door of the kitchen, followed closely by his younger brother, whose short legs churn in an effort to keep up. The older boy makes a game of it, running out of sight behind a cement wall and then into the dark *tienda*. His brother stops in the middle of the street, mystified. 'Juan!' he calls, the little voice plaintive, 'Where are you?' Thinking he hears footsteps further around a bend in the road, the toddler runs on towards the river.

———

She fell in love. With the country and with a young man in the village where she was billeted. When her obligation to the development agency was fulfilled, she stayed on and continued to teach at the local school. She'd already Latinized the spelling of her name, from Gabrielle to Gabriela. When many of the villagers shortened that to Gaby, she was pleased. It meant they felt comfortable with her, but also, indirectly, it was a small rebellion; her mother would never have approved. Alejo proposed. Gaby wrote, ecstatic, to her family, to invite them to the wedding.

Her mother refused to come.

The letter from her sister was like a sustained punch in the gut; reading it, she felt short of breath, a band of tension around her head, 'Well, she's furious of course. Really, what did you expect? Take my advice, come home and think it over. You may feel very differently about him when you're back in the States.' Almost as an afterthought, Constance had added, 'If he loves you, he'll wait.'

But I can't wait, thought Gaby, placing a hand on her belly. The pregnancy had taken her by surprise, but two months of queasy mornings and missed periods confirmed what Alejo's mother had already guessed.

'It is a blessing,' Ana had said, squeezing Gaby in a fierce hug, 'To be a grandmother. Your mother and I will rejoice together.'

Gaby burned the letter even though no one else in the village could read it, and told Alejo's parents her mother was too sick to make the trip. I have a new family now, she said to herself.

It was a modest wedding by American standards, taking place in the small wood-and-cane church that looked onto the village square. In childhood daydreams she'd imagined herself in a froth of white lace and tulle, coming out of a wooden archway and down a flagstone path between box hedges. Even her high-school feminism had done little to displace the fairy-tale picture. But the image wouldn't translate to the jungle, so she gave it up, along with her family's presence. Gaby had sewn a new dress for herself, sleeveless, white cotton. Her sisters-in-law had encouraged her to add ribbons, lace, sequins, they'd offered to paint her face and fingernails, frowned at her plain hair. 'A bride is as beautiful on her wedding day,' they protested, '*como un mariposa.*'

A butterfly? Gaby repeated to herself. The extravagance of the image embarrassed her. She still couldn't think like that, couldn't quite shed her North American reserve with its feminist disdain for the gewgaws and makeup favoured by these Latinas. But neither could she argue with her heart. Alejo made her feel beautiful, completely transformed from the plain shy woman she'd been when she first arrived. She'd joined the Peace Corps to escape her mother's house. Years under that critical eye had made her believe she had little to offer.

Here in Ecuador, in a village on the Rio Cononaco, everything was different because she was different, she was loved. Children clung to her in the street. Villagers regularly invited her to dinner. The whole community took pride in their English-speaking English teacher. '*Patrona*,' they said, and '*profesora*.' Alejo called her '*mi amor*'.

With willing resignation, she put herself into the hands of her *novio's* family. She let his sisters decorate her. Like a cake, she thought, when she spied the results in the one cracked mirror of his mother's house.

Into earlobes they had pierced with a needle weeks before, laughing at her shrieks, the sisters had slipped the thick gold stems of Ana's earrings. These were beautiful but baroque, antiques handed down in Ana's family, a floral design dripping with natural pearls. They painted her eyelids blue, 'because Alejo said your eyes are pieces of the sky.'

It made her want to cry with happiness. 'And he is my earth,' she told the women, immediately sheepish about the metaphor, its melodrama, but they smiled their approval.

'*Oye*, she sounds like one of us.'

She drew the line at the bright pink lipstick, then at the dark red, and finally at the almost purple, but allowed them to apply mascara to her pale lashes. They tucked a coral hibiscus into her braid and tied another to her wrist.

When she walked towards the front of the church on her father-in-law's arm, she thought her heart would burst. Alejo stood at the front of the pews, handsome, smiling. Maybe it was a trick of the light, the sun's rays streaming in from the windows at the side of the church, but for a moment he seemed surrounded by a golden aureole, angelic.

'Oh,' the single word escaped her lips. Beside her, her father-in-law turned an inquiring face toward her. She wondered if she was going to cry. Instead she took a deep breath, raised her head and continued without hesitation to the altar to take her place beside Alejo. Minutes from now he would be her life's partner. She looked into his face. He was so *guapo*, thick dark hair swept back from his face, beads of sweat standing out on the unlined brow, a dark shadow on his firm jaw though he had obviously just shaved. He was nervous too, yet his eyes on hers were loving, gathering her in.

You are my future, she thought.

The simple poverty of the church only added to her happiness. The choir consisted of a tape deck with obstinate buttons. Gaby had given the priest four new batteries and a tape to play as she and Alejo walked down the aisle. The priest punched the buttons, the scratchy sound of James Taylor accompanied them out onto the cracked cement steps. Alejo wiped the sweat from his forehead with a large handkerchief. He grinned at her and gave her waist a squeeze.

'Are you hungry, *mi señora?*' He was nodding toward the square and its almost miraculous transformation. Their wedding service hadn't taken more than an hour and yet a handful of villagers had set up tables, laid out food, and hung streamers and gaily coloured lanterns in the scrubby trees that bordered the street.

Long tables bore plates of fruit and cake. Two whole roasted pigs grinned from platters. There were platters of salad and *mote*, the white corn they called 'hominy' back home. There were plaintains halved and boiled, and bowls of *aji*.

Gaby felt tears spring to her eyes. In her entire upbringing, she'd never had a party, her mother hadn't approved of them. Family birthdays had been stiff affairs, a good meal, a new stiff dress, presents from an aging grandmother that required immediate acknowledgement in the form of a thank-you card. Depending on the birthday, Gabrielle or her sister were called to account for the past year, asked to predict accomplishments for the next. While Constance thrived on the regimen and often prepared a little speech, Gaby muttered, staring at her feet, twisting a linen napkin or perhaps knocking a piece of the heavy silver flatware to the floor. Invariably, she was cut short by her mother's imperious voice.

'What am I going to do with you, young lady?' A rhetorical question, it implied that nothing, nothing at all could be done.

Looking out at the streamers flicking in the light breeze, Gaby felt relief beyond words that her family's disapproval had expressed itself by their absence. For a moment she saw the scene before her through their eyes. The shiny dresses and smiling faces, the packed dirt of the square and the simple food laid out on long tables covered with sheets. To them it would be tawdry, even pitiful. She put her hands over her face to block out the vision.

'Are you feeling ill?' Alejo inquired, bending his head towards hers, his voice full of concern.

'Oh, no, *mi amor.*' She put her arms around his neck. 'I'm the happiest woman in the world,' she whispered in his ear. From behind them there came a small cheer and a burst of clapping.

'Kiss him,' someone suggested and the two young newlyweds smiled and did as they were asked, Alejo bending forward, Gaby dipping in his arms in a mock swoon.

'Be careful,' said Ana. 'You need your strength for later!' and with that the group laughed and descended the stairs to begin the celebrations.

The dancing and eating and drinking went on until long

after the bridal couple had retired. Gaby lay in her husband's arms after they had made love, too excited to sleep. She stroked his shoulder while he gently snored. Tomorrow they would begin their honeymoon journey. Nowhere in the world, she thought, is there anyone luckier than me. She could hear people walking by outside. In the moonlight streaming through the window, she looked down at the curving line of Alejo's body, covered by the pale sheet. Their clothing lay thrown over a chair in the corner. Someone went by in the street carrying something large, perhaps one of the tables. The shadow of it entered the window obliquely and swept in an arc across the room. The last thing she saw before she closed her eyes was her white dress swallowed in shadow, suddenly black. She fell asleep.

The next morning they boarded a wide raft, waving goodbye to his family on the dock. Their plans were to travel by river to a nearby town with road access. From there they'd flag a bus or car to get to a small city where they would stay overnight before continuing on to the capital. Gaby was giddy, laughing at everything.

'Oh, look, Alejo,' she exclaimed, pointing to an egret on the bank. It raised one leg slowly, paused and then tucked its beak under a wing to scratch. Alejo poled and the raft slid by the bird. Moments later a cloud of yellow-green rose with a screech from the trees, a flock of parrots.

Gaby clapped her hands, '*Loros!*' she called out. Alejo smiled, steering the raft into the centre of the river.

She leaned back and felt the sun on her face. 'Husband,' she said, grinning up at him, 'I think I'll have a little nap.'

'Sleep well, *mi amor*,' he said. She shut her eyes. The sound of the water sliding beneath the raft was soothing. At regular intervals she heard the pole being lifted, the tinkle of drops from along the length of it, the soft sucking as it was dipped again. She fell into a doze.

[ 42 ]

The jerk of the raft hitting something hard jolted her awake with a yelp. A convulsion shimmied through the wood beneath her. The raft seemed to buckle and suddenly, Gaby was lurching forward, losing her balance, grabbing for a handhold. Her fingers closed around a sliding duffel bag. 'Alejo!' she screamed. The shore and sky were arcing wildly. 'Oh, God,' she cried. 'Help!' She had enough time to gulp air before she went under, the dark water rising to engulf her. She felt rather than heard the fat slap of the raft as it came toppling over. Underwater, she swam, automatically aiming down and sideways to get out from under it. Her leg grazed something, a pole, an arm? She kept going until there was no breath left in her lungs. She surfaced, gasping.

She coughed, taking in breath, kicking her legs in circles to keep her head above water. 'Alejo?' No answer. Where was he? She splashed around in circles, staring wildly at the shore, up and down river. The raft was lodged upside down and at an odd angle, all but a corner of it underwater. One of the duffel bags bobbed out from under. She swam towards it, grabbed and pushed it up over the protruding corner, hooking its handle on one of the logs.

She hung onto the raft and called, 'Alejo, Alejo.' By now she was in a full-blown panic, knowing he was trapped, somehow, underneath the raft. She dove along the bound logs, arms reaching and grasping, head pounding with the pressure, searching for her husband in the dark water.

After several dives she was forced to rest. On the bank, she tried to massage warmth back into her trembling arms and legs. She was whimpering, moaning his name over and over. Swimming back out to the raft and diving again, she almost blacked out. The sun was dipping behind the trees when help finally arrived. Two men in a *canoa* motored slowly around the bend in the river. Gaby screamed at them for help. In her shock, she did not realize that she'd reverted to English.

'Alejo, where is he? Help me. I can't find him!' The men tied their canoe to a tree.

'Hurry!' she screamed as they stripped off their shirts and trousers. They took turns diving or restraining Gaby. She was close to hysteria and collapse, both. After an hour they tried to get her to return to town in their boat. She refused. The men had a muttered exchange. One of them stayed with her, his arm around her in the gathering dusk, while the other motored back along the river. Gaby rocked on her haunches, her voice sliding through the octaves of grief and fear, a thin trail of drool mixing with the tears on her chin. By the time the *canoa* returned from the village with two women, she was making an odd sort of humming noise, eyes wide and staring. It took the four of them to get her into the boat. She went momentarily berserk when they started the motor up. One of the women turned and slapped her across the face. Gaby whimpered, slumped forward, let herself be taken into the woman's embrace.

In town they carried her, delirious with exhaustion and shock, to her mother-in-law's home. Laid on Ana's bed, hearing the sounds of keening mixed with low voices in the main room, she fell into a troubled sleep. She dreamed she was dancing with Alejo in a room that slowly filled with water. Finally, her dream self watched as horses flew low over a winding river. She woke and dozed and woke again, feverish, confused, not knowing where she was.

Sometimes the sun came through the curtains. At other times it was dark. Had hours passed? Days? In the street outside she heard low voices. Dragging herself to the window, she saw people sitting in front of the house on benches. She did not understand who the vigil was for. Again, tiredness engulfed her, a wave washing over her and dragging her back to the bed.

She lost the baby a week later, miscarrying at four months.

With the blood draining onto rags pinned to her underwear, the last of what had held her to the world, the last desire to stay in it, was removed. She no longer cried, but lay in a darkened corner of the house she would have shared with Alejo, longing for the oblivion of sleep. Each time she awoke there was a moment when she forgot that everything had changed. A breeze rustling through the leaves of the *maté* tree, the cluck of chickens in Ana's yard next door, the smell of onions frying – something – would capture her attention, leading her to remember where she was. In that instant she felt the loss again, each morning a repetition of the one cruel fact: Alejo was dead.

She refused food and only left the bed to drag herself to the outhouse and back. Alejo's mother came daily.

Through a fog of grief she sensed Ana's presence. Sometimes she heard the older woman crying, softly, by her bed. Gaby heard the thunk of the machete on the chopping block, and though she was not aware of the weeks passing, perhaps it registered that there were fewer chickens scratching in the yard. Later she would be told that Ana had sacrificed half of her small flock, killing one a week, to make the fortifying broth she forced between Gaby's lips.

Gaby fainted one day, halfway across the yard, sinking almost gracefully into a velvet swoon. When she awoke she was back on the bed, a painful headache throbbing at her temples. Later, the soup that Ana spooned into her mouth made her shiver. The taste on Gaby's tongue was bitter, like roots or bark. She swallowed it compliantly. She did not know that Ana had consulted the local *bruja* or witch, and paid for a potion.

Every night, Ana sat by the bed with a cross held to her lips, whispering prayers. As Gaby sank into a deep almost drugged sleep, she sometimes felt Ana's leathery fingers on her brow, smoothing lank hair. She heard her mother-in-law's pleas, 'Do not give up, do not make me lose you too.' Gaby heard the pain and need in the older woman's voice but could not respond to it. She wanted to die. A great and suffocating weight had descended on her heart and lungs. She could only lie on the thin mattress, smelling the fusty odour of her own body and bedclothes.

Afterwards, she would hear that there came a point when Ana resolved to take more drastic action. Alejo's father went to the next village to fetch the one person there who could carry out the task. He returned with the missionary who helped to compose and then transcribe a letter to *la otra mama de Gabriela*.

Within six weeks of Alejo's death, Gaby sat occasionally in the yard. It was easier, at times, to acquiesce in Ana's encouragement. On a small wooden bench, Gaby blinked in the sunshine, feeling warmth on her hair and skin, a contradiction to the chill inside her. It had become something to guard, this void at the centre of her heart. The sound of children laughing in the streets was too raucous, like screeching parrots; their simple happiness made no sense. She had forgotten an entire repertoire of feelings.

And yet, at Ana's insistence, Gaby was now eating a small scoop of rice every afternoon. Sometimes, she detected another flavour, a bit of boiled fish, or the chopped white of a fried egg that had been hidden in the rice. Behind the veil of her depression, sensations of taste and touch came to Gaby as if from another dimension, so she did not think 'fish' or 'egg', she chewed and swallowed and was numb. But in spite of herself, she was regaining some physical strength.

The Gaby of old would have applauded and appreciated Ana's methods. These were the things that had drawn the gringa to the culture, that had made her willing to set aside her North American past. In this jungle village, people paid Death the homage they knew it deserved. Where Gaby's own mother would have told her to snap out of it, or arranged weekly visits with a psychiatrist, Ana ministered to Gaby's grief. Doing so was an expression of her own loss. Later, Ana would say, 'You were still married, my daughter. You were a spirit bride.'

Death made its claim on the living. You could only outwit it if you kept your victories small and humble, if you were willing to wait.

They had now embarked on a daily regimen of exercise. Each day as Gaby leaned on Ana's arm, she allowed herself to be propelled farther and farther along dirt tracks between the cane houses. Her surroundings were both familiar and strange, she moved like a sleepwalker, following Ana's lead, not aware that the older woman took special care to avoid even a glimpse of the river. To passersby they made an odd pair, the gringa half a foot taller than her companion, with clothes that hung scarecrow-slack on her thin frame. She walked like an old man, like something the wind might blow over.

One day, at noon Ana put in front of Gaby a fried fish, rice, a fried plantain and *ensalada de tomates*. Before Gaby knew what she was doing, she'd eaten the plate clean. Looking up from the table she saw the smile on Ana's face.

But Gaby remained silent. Since Alejo's death she had spoken only English and of that, no more than a mumbled 'no' or 'thank you' daily. There was no one in the village who could reach her in her own tongue. There was nothing in Gaby that wanted to be said.

In the prayers uttered every night at the bedside, she now heard Ana refer to a letter, she heard her mother-in-law pray for a swift reply. Like the vaguely registered events of the village, the sounds and smells coming in through the cane walls, this was one more element that Gaby absorbed without interest. She did not ask about it, but if she had, she would have been told, 'Two mothers are better than one.' She would have been told, 'I know your mother would want to know, I know she would want to send *su amor*, her love, *su fuerca*, her strength. Maybe she will even come.'

But when the letter finally arrives, with its undisguised scorn for everything Ecuadorian, Gaby will be grateful that its contents are indecipherable to her family here. She knows the letter would make no sense to Ana, who would wonder, What kind of woman drives her daughter away while she claims to want her back? When it finally comes, Gaby will read it in private and cry. To Ana, she will say, 'Thank you for letting her know.' She will add only, 'My mother is quite ill.'

She is out walking by herself for the first time, a twinge of jealousy at the happy commotion in Ana's kitchen. Drawn down the dirt road to the river, its inexorable pull.

Hearing the splash, she freezes. A child is calling, distressed. There is the sound of water slapping at the sides of the *canoas* and *bongos*. A shriek – *Mami!* – and then two sounds punch together, the thunk of something hitting wood, another splash. She's running, adrenalin surging through papery limbs, small puffs of dust coming up off the surface of the road as she careers around the last corner and down the short slope to where the village boats are moored. One of them is out there, drifting. There isn't anyone in it. Something's floating just off the bow of the *bongo*, a dome of wet white cotton, the dark mound next to it.

Alejo?

Gaby kicks her rubber thongs off and dives into the dark water. The memory of strength in her arms, her legs, stroke after stroke, head up, where is he? Propels her body forward, the drag of wet clothes around her torso and limbs. Reaches the *canoa*. Oh, please God, let me find him. Hanging onto the gunwale with her right hand and kicking circles, grazes something with her toe. Immediately plunges, eyes wide open in the murky water, arms moving in wide arcs, touches cloth, thrusts, the body shifting out of range again, swims underwater toward it, no breath left, where is he?

Up to the surface, gasping, coughing, gulping air. Down. Arms are frantic spirals, searching. Bubbles blooming from her nose and mouth, shirt rising to her chin, pulling it down with one hand when the other finds him. Grabs this time, fingers like pincers, yanks the cloth and what's in it toward her.

Up, up, the small body a slow stubborn weight, dragging her down as she tries to raise it. Desperate legs, pushing, kicking, lungs bursting. Into the air, spluttering, hand under his chin, other arm reaching for the *canoa*, no strength left. The wooden boat bouncing when she grips it, dipping and then an answering lift, tugging at her arm. She almost loses hold. A breathless scream from the back of her throat. Hooks her arm over the side of the *bongo*, the other cradling the boy, she knows it's a boy now, not Alejo, and the only thing in her mind is the need to breathe into him.

She bends in this awkward position towards his lips, starts the ventilations, but his mouth keeps slipping out from under hers. Tries bringing her right leg up under his body but his small legs slide down the inside of her thigh. Impossible. Curls the one hand around the face, closes it around his jaw, twists him around and pushes so that he drifts across in the brown water in front of her chest. She nudges the boy's shoulders with her own until his head is in the crook of her elbow.

She bends again towards his sweet blank face, squeezes the lips apart and into a skewed 'O', long-ago lessons at her high school pool flooding back. Breathe, pause, breathe, pause, breathe, Alejo? Breathe, pause, breathe. Loses track of time, is simply these lungs forcing air into the boy, breathe, pause, breathe. And he's suddenly coughing, spluttering, a jerking bundle of short limbs, thrashing, clawing at her.

She feels the sharp whack below her eye and moments later a small hand scratches down her face, drawing blood. He yanks at her hair, trying to pull himself out of the water. It's all she can do to keep hold of the boat, the other arm encircling his body, gathering the flailing limbs and terror in, saying over and over, '*Calma te nino, tranquilo, tranquilo.*' His panic subsides, now he's snuffling against her neck, and she's saying softly, 'You're alive, it's okay, thank you, God.'

'*Mami,*' he's whimpering, '*Mami.*' As if on cue, Gaby hears voices on the shore; someone is jumping into a boat; a motor flares to life. The sound expands, approaching. She feels the push of water as the boat draws up alongside. Strong arms take the child from her. Exhausted, she lets go of the *canoa*, almost goes under, feels a firm hand in one armpit, now the other, is hauled up and over the side.

All is confusion at first, back on shore. Mercedes, Ana's daughter, is almost hysterical with relief when her son is delivered into her arms. She hugs him to her chest, '*Gracias a Dios, gracias a Dios!*' Then she turns to Gaby.

'How could you take him out in the *canoa*, what were you thinking of? *Eres bruja*, witch, *matas todo que tocas*, you kill everything you touch. Stay away from my child!'

Gaby stares at her. Ana is just now running up, the baby in her arms, young Juan trotting behind her. She looks in alarm from one woman to the other, the maternal fury in her daughter's face, Gabriela's astonishment at the accusation. Slowly, in the perfect Spanish that earned her college honours, Gaby explains.

'He was out there already, in the river. I dove in. I couldn't see him at first. I found him finally, under the water. I pulled him up and,' here she pauses, as if unsure of how to express the rest. There are tears in her eyes, when she finishes, 'I *breathed* for him.'

'*Gracias a Dios*,' Ana whispers, echoing her daughter, and then quietly, '*Gracias* Alejo, goodbye my son.'

Her daughter's face crumples, she mutters, '*Desculpame*, sister, forgive me, you saved my boy,' and suddenly every-body is hugging and laughing and crying by the river. And Juan, in uncharacteristic generosity, gives his little brother the whole paper sack of *caramelos* and the toddler, still wet but quite recovered, and not entirely sure of what the fuss is all about, marches from person to person on the dock, offering candy. He shares his bounty with the men who pulled him from the river, who are now securing the *canoas*, he holds up the small sack to his brother, grandmother and mother, and finally, shyly, to his blond aunt.

'*Tia* Gaby,' he says, 'Why are you crying?' as she bends toward him, smiling through her tears.

He reaches up and traces the scratch on her cheek. He makes a noise like his grandmother might, a tut-tut of con-cern, then kisses his finger and touches it to the drying blood.

In a few days that letter will arrive and though it requests Gaby's immediate return to the States, in fact orders it, it will have the opposite effect. She will leave this tranquil place, retracing the steps that she and Alejo took and all of those they didn't on their honeymoon journey.

And Ana will travel with her, like a little river inside her, and sometimes Gaby remembers the wind blowing her shirt against her once skinny chest, the flat dirt tracks between the cane houses of the small town, clacking palm fronds, and the purple surprise of a jacaranda in someone's yard where she is leaning on the arm of a short brown woman, who smells like bread.

But there is that letter, creased and carried, a goad older

and stronger than Ana's fierce and uncluttered love. It will be the reminder of a kind of pressure that Gaby, in her dazed grief, put aside; like the tightly held reins at a horse's neck, it will rekindle her restlessness. She will travel into her future, and live, pause, breathe, pause, and never find another Alejo, only her mother, everywhere she looks, in every man's heart.

# Eating *Cuy*

KWEE. That's the way it sounds, the name for guinea pig in Spanish. It's smaller than a cow, less work to feed and easier to slaughter. It's smaller than a rabbit, which many people refuse to eat on the grounds that something so cuddly shouldn't end up roasted and carved on a platter. *Cuy* is equally soft, and has the same innocent and inquisitive appearance with its twitching nose and button eyes. It should be a pet, she thinks, admiring its longish grey-beige coat. But it's what's for dinner if you're overnighting in Huaca. Pronounced *wha-ka*.

Huaca is cold and beautiful. Laid out around the town, as throughout the Andes, are plots of farmed land, patchwork velvet in every imaginable green and gold undulating across the slopes of these old mountains. Because it's cold but not freezing, the plants are happy, displaying what appears to be a perpetual state of bud or blossom. And the people glow as well, all surfaces kissed and shining in the moist chill air. It is only the foreigner, in thick sweater and long pants, who shivers at the sight of bare-legged women and children and wishes there were a bus, tonight, back to the somewhat more civilized and surely warmer city of Ibarra, which she and her new friend Celia left this morning.

But it is afternoon, and the plans they came with have been swept away. For hormones and sentimentality. Not hers, of course. No. After a day of being peripheral, of being cold-shouldered back onto the sidelines whenever she's attempted any incursion into the warm glow of Celia and Napo's togetherness, the foreigner is having what she fully recognizes as peevish thoughts. Self-pitying. The hours with Napo have taken their toll.

The rattling bus labours over the mountain highway. Celia, proud tour guide in the aisle seat, points over her friend's shoulder at the rolling hills and small towns that pass by their streaked window. This is the experience the foreigner has been hungry for without knowing it. Finally, exposure to the land and the people. Up until now she's spent too much time in the company of other tourists, working in the tiny boutique on a cruise ship in the Galapagos – forty-five days of T-shirts and suntan lotion, of catered meals and entertainment. But she'd met and made her first Ecuadorian friend.

For the last two days in Ibarra, the foreigner has enjoyed easygoing Latina hospitality: a tour of the market where Celia's mother has a stall; a *paseo* to a small village hosting a bullfight, even the funeral of a family friend. And now this trip by bus into the mountains. They are going partway to the Colombian border, to visit Celia's cousins, Raoul and Napo, short for Napoleón.

(All he needs is the satin waistcoat and the rearing horse. All he needs is a campaign, several hundred soldiers and a sworn adversary. And failing that, a stand-in or captive audience, a foreigner.)

'*Llegamos*,' Celia says suddenly, rising from her seat into the aisle, 'We've arrived.'

The bus pulls off the road onto the shoulder in a grind of gears. The two women scramble to the door and jump to gravel from its metal steps. An unpaved road angles away from the highway. Celia heads up this now.

A belch of black exhaust signals the departure of their bus. Staring after it, the foreigner wonders why she suddenly feels so abandoned. What possible advantage could be offered by its cracked plastic seats and the ripe odours of other passengers? By the incessant *cumbia* beat blaring from the tape deck above the driver's head?

The music trails back to them now, off-key and thinning in the mountain air.

Whoo. This is one high-up town. Her lungs heave in her chest. She assumes Celia is unaffected, but when she stops and turns, her eyes are wide. And there are two spots of colour high on her cheeks.

'Napo,' Celia is saying, 'is' – now a pause, as if the next part of the sentence won't form itself – 'my best friend,' she finishes lamely.

But there's nothing platonic in the electricity pulsing between the cousins at the door of his flat. The man who opens the door pulls Celia toward him and buries his face in her full hair. They stand like that for a long time. The foreigner doesn't know where to look. Only when Celia gently pulls free does Napo acknowledge the presence of a third party.

'And the gringa,' he says, casting a cool look in her direction.

Celia is speaking rapidly. The foreigner, hesitating in the doorway, can't understand a word of it. Napo interrupts the recitation, says distinctly, '*Vamos a ver.*' We'll see.

What? wonders the foreigner. What will we see?

Inside, he waves them both to take a seat around a low table and offers tea, plugging in a small kettle placed on the cement floor. The cousins are instantly talking.

The foreigner turns her attention to the flat, one large room bisected by an enormous glass-fronted bookshelf. The walls are painted blue and stained with damp. An unshaded lightbulb hangs from a stiff cord over the area where they sit, she and Celia to one side of the table on a small couch with Napo perched across from them on a wooden crate.

The conversation might be one left off months ago, but the cousins have picked it up with ease. The foreigner can't grasp any of it. For her, Celia has always spoken slowly, sometimes attempting a sentence or two in heavily accented English. What fills the room now is a sound poem, words and sentences flowing into each other, his overlapping hers, strung together like chains, binding them, excluding the gringa.

But, she reminds herself, they haven't seen one another in ages.

The kettle is boiling. Napo takes a couple of tea bags from a tin and drops them into two of the three cups he has arranged on the table in front of his knees. When these have been filled with hot water and steeped, he removes the bags and pushes one across to Celia, pulling the other towards himself. One of the used teabags is dumped in the remaining cup. He pushes this, the bag still in it, toward the foreigner. She has to reach for the spoon, getting up off the couch to do so. '*Gracias*,' she says, careful not to let sarcasm enter her voice. Napo pauses, looks at her.

'You're not cold?' asks the foreigner, surprised into participating in the conversation. Napo is wearing only a wool shirt and jeans.

One dark eyebrow is raised. In beautifully enunciated Spanish, at one third of the speed with which he's been talking up until now, he replies, 'The people who live here are not afraid of the cold. When I am away from Huaca for any time, my body needs to re-acclimatize. I do that by wearing only a T-shirt for several weeks.'

Like Eskimo babies, thinks the foreigner, naked in igloos. If she could think of the words in Spanish to describe this she would, but Napo isn't listening. He's drained his cup and now he's standing, a signal that he's ready to go out.

From the flat they walk towards the church, its bell tower rising above the village square. Looking out over clay roofs she sees patches of sun, handkerchiefs of light, roving the slopes of distant peaks. Between these and the town the land ripples, row upon row of supine giants – green buttocks, green thighs and breasts.

On the bus ride up, Celia had talked of Napo's work. After university he'd returned to town, applied for government funding and opened a community centre. He's describing it now as well as the cultural programs he administers: a dance troupe, a small theatre company, a tiny museum and library.

They enter the market in a courtyard beside the church, accessed through a wide gateway at the top of the street. Low tables covered with vegetables share space with small flat wagons. Some of the vendors sell off the ground, seated on flattened sacks next to small hills of potatoes and conical mounds of peas, corn or beans. Legs stretched in front of them, the women knit or weave fine bags from cactus fibres. The air smells of earth, of lemon grass and *cilantro*. Napo is a low-key politician, shaking hands, chatting with everyone. Celia is greeted warmly, welcomed back. Only when someone asks for an introduction is the foreigner presented.

From the market they walk in a wide circle of the town and she hangs back a bit, taking pictures. They stop in a dark bar for a cup of tea and for the duration of their rest, she fends off the benign advances of an old and toothless fellow who squats near her chair. Outside the doorway three young boys kick a soccer ball back and forth.

Napo is talking, his arm loosely around his cousin's shoulders; Celia interjects on occasion, especially when the subject is music. She is a singer; her rich contralto voice had awed the foreigner when she first heard it on the cruise ship.

'*La musica es la sangre de la gente*,' she is saying.

The blood of the people, translates the foreigner, silently. That's beautiful.

'*La sangre caliente*,' Napo agrees.

[ 57 ]

Hot blood, it's how they think of themselves, a warm and passionate people. And yet capable of icy disdain when it suits them.

She has already offered the usual disclaimer, 'Forgive me, I don't speak the language very well.' The charming and disarming admission. But Napo hasn't smiled, or encouraged her with compliments on her accent. He doesn't seem to need to hear from her at all. This is a lecture; she's expected to pay attention.

'Our culture needs to be kept alive. We must fight against the influences of *el mundo primero*.' He says these last words sarcastically.

When they continue their walk, Napo picks up the pace. Patting her chest, the foreigner comments on the altitude and immediately wishes she hadn't.

Now he is enumerating the negative influences on his country: commercialism, television, the greed of oil companies. She nods in agreement. But the word that comes into her head is French – *d'accord*. She doesn't offer it.

They stop where the road divides. A volleyball game is in process, the net stretched perpendicular to the side of a two-storey building. Stained along its base with dirt, the wall is covered with a large simple mural. Against a wash of red, a pair of hands, pink, reach toward the sky. A stylized dove floats above them. Underneath, a partially obliterated message reads, '*Si amas la vida*,' If you love life ...

Two young boys go by on horseback. They stare at her, solemn-faced, then ride on. Further up the road they begin to laugh. The sound of it drifts back to her, punctuated by the tock-tocking of hooves on stone, men breathing in and expelling air, fingers popping against a ball, the grunts and expletives of the game. Napo's voice is insistent, compelling. Even when she wants to ignore him, she can't. He's an attractive man and knows it. But it's more than that; she's playing a part he's designed for her.

Movies. Drugs. The one English word he uses repeatedly, 'junkies'. Minutes later she realizes she's misheard, that he's denouncing North Americans. She's on trial, isn't she, for the uses and abuses of this lovely country by the hated 'yankees'? He says it again, in an accent as thick and chewy as gum, he says it pejoratively, his speech has been peppered with it.

No, she wants to say, you're wrong, I'm not the enemy.

From behind them, they hear a shout. In the doorway of a yellow house, just off the road that slopes toward the highway, a man waves.

'*Mi otro primo*,' says Celia. The other cousin.

The man ducks into the shadowed interior of his house and then re-emerges. His voice reaches up to them with an invitation to come and eat.

Food. Something warm. And a break from this.

They tramp down the dirt road to the house. Inside, after introductions, and the flurry of hands and cutlery and bread and bowls of steaming soup that accompany the beginning of their meal, the conversation shifts. The cousins are catching up on each other's lives. Raoul is a larger version of his brother, with a broad, kind face. His wife is petite, pretty, her dark hair swings forward as she bends over a wicker bassinet placed beside her chair. The baby gurgles.

The foreigner bends over her bowl. The soup is delicious, a thick purée of squash with seasonings her palate does not recognize. Soon, she thinks, soon we'll be on our way; they'd agreed this morning, 'We'll be back by midnight.'

Celia is clapping her hands, delighted, and suddenly everyone is looking at the foreigner, expectant.

'*Como?*' she asks. How? Meaning what. Napo laughs, not kindly, and mimics her, '*Como, como?*'

'We're going to have *cuy*,' says Celia. 'Tonight.'

'But we don't want to miss our bus back,' says the for-eigner, looking in alarm at her friend.

'So North American, watching your watch,' says Napo. Celia laughs.

'Sticking to schedules,' Napo goes on. 'Very important in *Los Estados Unidos.*'

'*Soy Canadiense,*' the foreigner retorts, feeling the prickle of tears at her eyelids. 'There's a difference.'

Across the table, Raoul's wife nudges him.

'We'll go to the highway,' he says. 'We can try for a bus.'

But there is no bus, at least, not for her. For half an hour the four of them – Raoul's wife has stayed behind with the baby – stand at the side of the highway. It's the main route to the Colombian border. Vehicles fly by at speeds she finds capricious for these mountain roads. The men wave at the buses. She and her friend wave too. The buses are full. None of them stop.

They tramp back up a steep incline, away from the high-way. She appreciates Raoul's kindness, and has resigned her-self to the change in plans. Okay. *Cuy* it is.

*La invitada de honor.* This is how Napo now refers to her. At times he even mock-bows, sweeping an arm across the space in front of her as they pass others on the road. '*Buenas tardes,*' say the smiling people they encounter. '*Ola gringa!*' shouts a young boy, giggling. The altitude presses against her lungs and squeezes her thigh muscles. Her feet, in cotton socks, are freezing.

*Cuy.* The woman up the road raises them in a pen. Her kitchen is a mud-walled room off the house, thick walls black with the smoke of every fire she has cooked over. The for-eigner can't imagine life like this, cooking in a kitchen like this. Her own white and pristine past is deflating like a bal-loon, whistling its rubbery breath in her ear, memories of clean tiled surfaces, gleam and chrome. *Cuy.* The woman puts the handful of ancient leathery notes, the price for two, in her cotton apron. Napo says something that makes her smile. Out of the indoor gloom an old man appears in the doorway. The woman takes his arm and leads him to a chair in the thin sunshine. Cabbages and onions fill a small garden plot surrounded by a built-up wall of earth. Spiky sisal bushes crown the wall like a row of giant pineapple tops, nature's fencing.

Napo carries one of the guinea pigs. The other nestles in the large hands of Marco, a friend of Napo's they've picked up on the road. Walking to the rear of their little group is Marco's fair-haired girlfriend. The foreigner smiles at her.

'Do you speak English?'

'*Nein.*'

A guinea pig at the beginning of a story – which one? One of the Narnia books. An old association. Anthropomorphism, she cannot avoid it, thinking of all animals as they first appeared to her in bedtime stories wearing little hats and leaning on canes in tidy sitting rooms hollowed out of tree trunks. A kettle whistling on the hob. Small tables laid for tea. All this conjured up by the sight of the dear sniffling *cuy*, one dark, the other pale as palomino, as they are carried from their point of purchase to their slaughter.

Back at Napo's place, the *cuy* are dispatched immediately, their throats slit by the woman who rents Napo his rooms. The skinning and disembowelling are fast, efficient, Napo and his landlady side by side. Buckets of water sluice the blood down the drain of the courtyard. The entrails are the landlady's to fry for her family, red-black livers and blue-brown hearts. A bit of gristle for the dogs who sniff and snap, and are finally locked in a pen at the back of the court-yard.

The flesh of the *cuy* is pink, pretty. Someone lights the brazier.

There is an hour or so to pass while the wood burns down to coals. Napo goes off on an errand. For warmth, Celia and her friend now huddle under quilts at opposite ends of the mattress in the tiny sleeping chamber behind the bookshelves. They have mugs of *guayusa*, an herbal tea, spiked with cane liquor.

Heads poke around the corner of the bookshelves, people who'll be coming for dinner, with offers of bread or wine. In a half hour the two women will go into the kitchen, they'll scrub potatoes and boil them in a big blackened pot. They'll make a salad of tomatoes, cabbage and *cilantro*, squeezing two lemons over it and then a shake of salt. It will be passed from hand to hand around the brazier, finger-scooped into mouths, no cutlery tonight, no standing on ceremony in this communal celebration.

For now they are trading stories with Napo's friend José, a dancer possessing a charming smile and massive, sculpted thighs who has happened along and is snuggling in under the coverlet. He will come tonight, he will bring his wife. The foreigner sighs; Napo's temporary absence is a relief, the sudden proximity of bodies a pleasant surprise. Legs bump legs; she rubs her feet back and forth against the mattress and the chill leaves her toes. The all-Spanish conversation is lulling her into a kind of sweet quiescence because they have started to sip the hot *aguardiente*, and are talking about art and life, two subjects which calm her even as they raise, in her, a passionate response.

'*Soy pintura*,' she says to José, I'm a painter. For the first time all day she can pretend to a certain eloquence in the language, she can even pretend she belongs. At least this is a house, a home. She has been away so long from anything she could call home that a warm bed and warm conversation offer themselves as a temporary substitute. She is relieved to have the intimacy back with Celia, who winks when José gets up to leave, who whispers '*Que cuerpo* – what a body,' when the dancer is gone.

And now Celia is sharing confidences about Napoleón, 'He changed my life,' she says simply. 'My whole approach to music – I was young, foolish; I sang the popular songs from the radio. All about love and romance,' she grimaces. 'I wore make-up all the time, and wanted fancy clothes.' She takes a sip from her steaming drink. 'Napo introduced me to the reality of my people. He opened my ears. I started to listen to the real singers, Victor Jara, Mercedes Souza. I learned to sing from a true heart.'

'Ah,' says the foreigner, snuggling under the overblown roses of the comforter. A photo of a much younger Celia smiles at her from the low crate at the side of the bed.

'He was the most important influence on my music,' Celia says this vehemently, as if somebody needs convincing. 'But I had to leave, to learn to be independent.'

'Mm-hmm,' says the foreigner.

'So I ended up in the Galapagos.' Since their meeting on the ship, Celia has talked excitedly about her plans to go to the States. 'He never wanted me to leave,' her voice has dropped to a whisper, 'And now I am going away again.'

The foreigner says, 'Ah,' and then, 'I see,' because, though it has taken her these many hours, she does.

After the *cuy*, and more and more of the *aguardiente*; after the plaintive, romantic and rousing songs, '*Gracias a la vida*' and '*Comandante Ché*'; after José has become insensate from drink and theatricality, leaning heavily on everyone's shoulders and crying about his sad life and pregnant mistress; after his wife has all but carried him, weeping, home; after the sad German woman and her sour-faced lover have left, Celia will return to this bed.

But the *cuy*. They are a startling centrepiece to the drunken, emotional evening. Around a small brazier, on chairs, the yellow and red plastic crates called *javas*, and one overturned bucket, the dinner guests gather, like fans at the track. No longer fat and furry, the *cuy* grow bronze above the heat of the coals, their rodent bodies arching on long sticks, open mouths spreading wide and wider in a heat-strained grimace, miniature greyhounds, limbs taut to the race. Screaming silently and ghoulishly above the coals, flying straight and fast and true as racing dogs across the white ash and red glow of the fire, through the crisp, chill air.

The foreigner eats. A tiny drumstick, a piece of sweet flesh from the breast. Even as she is horrified by their twin heat snarls, even though she calls herself a vegetarian, she knows while they are baking brown over the coals – she is going to eat *cuy*. She has no real will at this altitude. No real identity. She is simply the foreigner, the one to whom less and less attention has been directed throughout the day and night. She eats *cuy* to feel less transparent. She eats *cuy* to have bulk in her stomach, her bowels, otherwise she fears she's made of air, hollow as a straw, something to suck through and discard.

Across the courtyard and up one flight of stairs from the room where the cousins talk and touch late into the night, the foreigner is assigned a bed. A guttering kerosene lamp lights her way to the borrowed room. She feels blank, blind, tinny with cold and weightlessness when she turns the crank that snuffs the wick. Sleep does not come at first and then only fitfully. She is angry, the smell of roasted *cuy* blooming from under the covers all night, from her clothes and hands, from her dreams. She needs to pee but does not want to venture out to find the cold stone-floored bathroom off the courtyard in the dark.

*La invitada de honor.* The excuse to come today. And tomorrow, the reason to leave. Beneath blankets that offer weight without comfort, she turns on the skewer of her difference, burdened by it, in this cold-blasted town, all through the cold, cold night.

She has a smart-ass friend back home who asks her, 'Did you find yourself?' after any trip she's taken, even a weekend away in cottage country. And all she can offer in reply is a certain rhythm in the thing she's been able to take for granted until now, traipsing through other people's village squares, their markets and churches, staring through windows and doorways, staring over hedges and over shoulders. She glimpses what eludes her, the thing that is always there but never attainable, impossible to share, because to share means to stay, to stop. For now she is defined by movement; she carries her difference like a badge, the backpack and blond ponytail, the substandard grasp of the language. This trip like all the trips before and after it.

On the bus back to Ibarra with Celia, so many people crammed in the aisle, the nuances of indignity impossible in the half languages they share, the foreigner is afraid to give offence, unable to explain why she feels so used, not yet willing to accept what Huaca has taught her, that the cultural gap is wide and strong and exists because she brought it with her.

With time though, resentment fades. Huaca remains in her memory, a chill jewel nestled in green velvet, a pink adobe wall adorned with the white dove of peace, a game of volleyball between the boys and men of neighbouring villages. Marx and Mao and Garcia Marquez behind the locked glass fronts of Napo's shelves and Celia's picture beside Napo's bed. José's thighs and José's tears. And the silent screams and bronzing skin, the taste and smell and sound and sight and symmetry of roasting *cuy*.

# Nickname

SHE'S WALKING by the henhouse when she hears, from inside, sounds of a commotion. Is it a *zorro*? She's lost chickens this way before, to an animal that looks like a fox. Shit. And no stick to bang on the outside of the hen house. No worker around to help her out. But my chickens, she thinks, I have to do something. And just as it dawns on her that a *zorro* is nocturnal and wouldn't be hunting in the middle of the day, she finds herself reacting in panic. A man. Coming out of the doorway. Longita's son? Stumbling out of the dusty, acrid gloom, one hand on his zipper, the other held up as if to ward off a blow.

The way I heard it first, the way she told it – she had no idea what was going on. What she'd interrupted. Not until she was down at the dock and the men – embarrassed and amused – spelled it out for her. But that's getting ahead of her tale. And Nicky is so good at telling stories.

Longita's son – whose name I learned but promptly forgot, remembering only the nickname that attached itself to him after the incident – scrambling like an animal pursued out of its warren. He's running now, slipping down the hill behind the stout stilts of the large cane house, finally crashing into the bush at the base of the slope. Sounds of his crazy progress drift up to Nicky long after she's lost sight of him, staring stunned at the two deep gouges he's carved into the hill, skid marks of his mad descent.

She enters the small *caña* shed, waits for her eyes to adjust. The hens are fussing, clucking, pecking at each other. One of them isn't moving. Is, in fact, dead; still warm but disembowelled after a fashion, pink entrails protruding from under its tail. She panics. Grabs the dead hen and runs, not in the direction taken by the fleeing man but down the south slope of the hill to the path that leads along the dikes surrounding the shrimp ponds to the loading dock. Her husband is working with two friends, a Brit and an American. They are fixing one of the boat motors. She is in a state – breathless and gasping, tears streaming down her face, when she arrives at the cement dock.

'My best hen,' she blurts out, crying in earnest now, like a baby, great gulps of air punctuating her speech, 'my hen, my best hen.'

The chicken's legs dangle uselessly, its head flopping to the side, one tiny eye open and glazed, gazing heavenward, and the other – as if conspiratorial in its own demise – closed; a final wink. The men begin to laugh, reading between the lines; one of them throws back his head and crows. The hen's neck is a rubbery tube in Nicky's fist, pink organs bounce as she brandishes the bird at her friends, whose response bewilders her. She is near hysteria. Small arcs of blood spray onto the cement.

Nicky doesn't know yet. She doesn't know that if you wring a chicken's neck, spasms and contractions will twist throughout its intestinal system as it dies. Providing stimulation to anything inside the chicken. She doesn't know and so she is inadvertently playing this absurd game of show and tell. Showing her dead hen to the men, who know that it's a case of bestiality. The men know, and cannot help their laughter, are amused even as Nicky slumps to the ground, tears streaming from her red nose onto her crossed rubber boots. She's cradling the hen, staring at it, when the puzzle of its body is explained by the Brit, confirmed by the American, and the sound from her mouth, her hand flying up to stifle it, is the horror of finally understanding. It wipes the embarrassed smiles off the men's faces. Her husband bends down to her, gently pries the bird loose from her grip, offers his arm. She leans on him heavily all the way back up to the house.

He pours her a strong drink. Leads her to the hammock on the veranda, kisses her wet cheek, picks the dead bird up from the railing where he laid it when they opened the cane gate of the porch and, walking around behind the house, starts down the hill.

Later that evening, over rum watered with more tears, Nicky laments the loss. The pain suffered by the bird, and hers, imagining its death, is what she buries first – so many years in this country, without a hard edge, you don't survive. It's easier to focus on the unlaid eggs; the hen was her most productive, her 'best'. And there's the meal they will not have. Any other bird dying in this yard would end up in the pot, chicken a rare treat in the steady diet of shrimp. But not this one. 'That fucker,' she says. Then, in spite of crying and due to the fourth rum before her on the table, when it might be observed that she is rather enjoying the drama of it all, Nicky giggles and says, 'That chickenfucker'. And so Longita's son becomes known as the Chickenfucker.

I meet him almost a year after the event, when he helps to push the boat out one sun-saturated morning, along the deep muddy channel that connects the shrimp farm to the river. I'm down for a visit from my job in Quito, teaching English as a foreign language.

It's Thanksgiving, there are six of us going on a picnic to an island farther south. We'll head for town first to pick up beer, cheese and bread. *Cervesas. Queso.* It's already noon and we're impatient but there's not enough tide yet to float the boat to the spot where the channel floor drops away. We're sinking knee-deep in mud, trying to manoeuvre the Boston whaler towards the bay. It's slow going. The mood is souring.

The smiling youth appears out of the mangrove alongside the channel and calls out *saludos* to the group. He offers to help, lays down his machete, steps neatly out of his boots, rolls his pants above the knee and hops into the thick mud. In English I ask, 'Who is this?' Someone whispers a reply. 'Who?' Shocked. 'Shh, we'll tell you later.'

He's got the compact musculature typical of the area. Ropy arms, small hips. Broad features in an almost ugly face. Lives with his mother, the tiny woman affectionately named Longita, in a little cane house in the rainforest behind the shrimp farm. Father unknown and long gone. They are one of the poorest families around and with the exception of this man's sister – pretty Bibiana with her own fatherless family – illiterate. Longita knows the saints' days of the calendar year, rattles off seven saints for any given week, lists a month of saints at a time and only stalls twice in a recitation of the annual list, 365 saints, *Gracias a Dios*. She knows the secrets of the woods as well, which leaf to press to a fevered forehead, which bark to brew for coughs, this dried plant mixed with the yolk of a day-old egg for rheumatism, this one burned in the four corners of a house to rid it of unwanted ghosts. The boy should marry soon but won't. Some say he's slow, 'Not all there.' He was the last of her children, born after she thought her womb had given up. Even before the incident, she'd shake her head when she mentioned his name.

Within minutes we've pushed the boat to the right spot. The story is saved until after our full-out sprint across the bay, until after the boat is anchored, the cooler of beer buried in the wet sand at the wave edge and we're sitting in the tepid shallows on our picnic island.

Nicky unwinds her tale like a maestro, the narrative fuelled by brief interjections from her husband Dan, who has stationed himself further up the slope of beach and is now layering sand by the wet handful over his outstretched legs. The others have wandered off, collecting shells; they've heard this one before. 'You tell the rest,' she says, when she's reached the point of her collapse into the swinging hammock. I'm disbelieving, imagination struggling against propriety.

Over and over my mind reverses to the beginning, filling in the parts that Nicky couldn't see or know. It's an insistent film, playing itself out: Longita's son in the chicken shed, his body and hands in shadow, the chickens squawking, footsteps through the grass, his face turning toward the avenue of sunshine from the shed's doorway, his actions blurred and manic when he realizes someone is outside, the wild explosion of his escape out of the tiny shed. I see him running until he reaches the safety of the forest and running still, slipping and sliding down the bush-festooned slope, swinging by one cupped hand round a fruit-bearing tree, a sweet fug in his nostrils from the overripe and fallen fruits beneath his feet. One leap across the river to the smooth washing stone at its centre, another to the opposite bank, up the slick clay path to a way between the trees that even now, in the beginning of the dry season, needs to be cleared of creepers daily. Running until he sees the tiny cane house, the oil drum at its corner that catches runoff from the roof, right through the tiny clearing where Longita's hens stoop and pick and now scatter in a screech at his drumming feet, into the bush again until he stops, gasping, lungs pounding, and collapses against a tree, adrenalin draining away painfully. He stares unseeing back at the house, back in the direction he came from.

Where Longita finds him, minutes later, on her return from foraging for nightshade. He does not tell her what is wrong, only that, by now, he realizes his machete is not with him, is instead where he put it down, just inside the entrance to the chicken shed. Longita stares at her son, who in turn is staring straight ahead through the thicket of bushes at nothing, at his own fear perhaps, or at a scene playing and replaying behind his eyes. She cuffs him once on the back of the head, not too hard, walks through the clearing into her house, lays the plant she's found on the tiny wooden table, touches the cross at her neck and heads down the path toward the shrimp farm.

'I met her at the river,' says Nicky's husband, Dan, picking up the story, 'She was coming to get his machete.

'Well, you know Longita. She greeted me and asked about my health and Nicky's health. I said we were both fine – well, Nicky's upset – I said. I was starting to feel nervous, I mean, I really had no plan when I started down to their house, I was mad I suppose, determined to teach him a lesson. Maybe I was going to make him pay for the chicken, penalize him in some way, tell him he couldn't work at the farm for a while, I don't know.' Dan sounds perplexed even now, responding all over again to a situation he would have preferred to avoid.

'I hadn't even thought about Longita,' he continues, 'and there she was in front of me on the path, this little old woman who's done so much for us. I had the hen in my hand, was holding it like this,' he gestures with his right hand off to the side, a sheepish look on his face. 'I think I said his name, her son's name, and then, I didn't know what to do, I was just holding the dead bird and standing there like an idiot.

'She stared at it for a while and then I said she could get the machete. We both knew where he'd left it.' He pauses in his story and for a moment surveys the sand landscape he has built around his legs. 'She reached out her hand for the chicken and laid it gently on the ground without looking at me.

'I muttered something, I don't remember what. She hadn't looked at me this whole time. Then I said – look, I'll get the machete, you wait here – and she said no, she needed to see the *señora*, to make her apologies. I said – oh, Longita, it's not your fault! – I mean we still hadn't, you know, talked about the way the hen died.' He pauses, mired in euphemism. All the while he's clawing at the beach, his fists closing around clumps of wet sand at his side.

'Anyway,' he continues, 'she gave me this look, fierce, kind of, or proud, and she said, *He's my son* – and then she shook her head, the way she always did,' he pauses, and it could be that he's remembering that moment, the prick of sweat at his collar, his discomfort. 'She led the way back up to the house.'

'All she said to me,' Nicky speaks up, 'was – *nunca, señora, nunca*, this will never happen again – and then she said she would pay for the hen. I started to protest, I mean Longita has no money, no work except what she occasionally does for us. She wouldn't be talked out of it, though.'

She glances over her shoulder at her husband, his legs still encased in sand. 'You're right, she looked so, mmm, power-ful. Determined. And then she got the machete and went back home.'

'We don't know what she did with the chicken,' Dan pauses. 'It wasn't something we could ask about.'

'Longita's done some wild things to people,' Nicky laughs, 'I figure anything's possible. Maybe she nailed the hen to his bed while it rotted, or smeared parts of it on his pillow and let him live with it for a while. No, that would mean she'd have to live with it too, the stink of it in the house.' Unlike Dan, Nicky is savouring the tale, showing it off. 'Oh, I know, I bet you she cooked it. Made him eat it – the whole thing. Yuck.

'Anyway, she came to the house every day for a month after that and cleaned and cooked for us and wouldn't take any money and finally I just said, "Longita, you've paid for the hen!" – and she said, no, *señora*, not yet, but I could tell she was tired. Before this she'd only worked two or three days a week for us.

'Gradually, she let us start paying her again.' Nicky smacks at a sand flea on her arm. 'When she let us give her a small bucket of shrimp, I figured it was over. We didn't see the Chickenfucker for three months at least, did we, honey?'

Dan sighs. 'Nope,' he replies. Heaving himself out of his sand bed, he stands upright and brushes the grit from his thighs and shins. As he walks toward the water, pellets of sand dislodge themselves from his creased shorts. They bounce on the hard beach. He wades in up to his waist and then dives.

Nicky's eyes are closed now, head tilted back, face bare to the sun. We sit in silence for several minutes. I'm watching Dan. He's way out, a small brown dot swimming through a field of silver. Nicky stirs, takes a last sip of the beer that she's canted into the sand at her side. 'Whaddya say' – she winks at me, a raconteur delighted by her own punch line – 'chicken for dinner?'

I don't see Dan and Nicky for a long time. At Easter, one of my students offers me a ride to the coast. I shed layers all the way down the mountain, stuffing first jacket, then sweater, then socks into my duffel bag as we descend into green soupy heat. I lean my head out the window as we come into Muisne, smiling at the barefoot kids who run, for a while, beside the car. It's sunset, too late to go anywhere. I stay overnight and arrange for a boat to the farm in the morning.

The *canoa* drops me at the far edge of the property. I sink halfway up my shins in the stinking mud. The tide is still out. Nicky waves from the packing area, shouts something I can't hear. She turns to dispatch a worker, someone to carry my bag and help me through the mud.

There's an art to this, but it's one I've never mastered. I've seen women in pretty dresses and shiny black pumps walk a gangplank from a crowded ship to a muddy bank, slip off their shoes and pick their way daintily to a higher, drier spot. They don't hesitate or, miracle of miracles, get dirty.

Not a speck of the slippery grey muck on their full cotton skirts or slim brown legs. I feel huge and North American, stranded in the mud in my rubber thongs, afraid to venture from this perch, the twin mud pits in which my feet are mired, captive. Nothing to do but wait. The men in the *canoa* bid me a laughing farewell. The worker is on his way. He's got a pair of rubber boots in one hand.

It's the Chickenfucker. And so this makes the second time he has come to my aid, striding gracefully through the mud. He greets me. Tactful, polite. I have to lean on his arm to rinse my feet in the channel before putting on the boots. He carries my bag slung over one shoulder as if it weighed no more than a feather pillow. He offers the other arm as support. We move slowly, aiming toward the distant loading dock where Nicky and Dan and a handful of their workers are going about the daily business. My hands are sweaty, already smeared with mud. The skin of his arm is smooth and firm. I know the sensations running rampant in my body. I know the lick of lust that grips me when he turns to lift me over a fallen tree in our path, hanging my bag on one of its branches momentarily so that he has both arms free to carry me over the log. I know he feels none of this, is simply doing his job, helping the clumsy visiting gringa. There is a slope now and he heads down first, positioning his body so that I can slip down after him, leaning into him to avoid falling. I'm dizzy with desire and effort. I am the expatriate, the outsider, pried open by the sensual nature of this country, astounded by its impact on me, by the impact of this young man who I always refer to in my mind, even as I hate myself for it, as the Chickenfucker, offering me his arm, his shoulder, his body as support. The offer is kind, routine. The *manglar* stinks more in some places than others, a smell of rotting eggs. It's Easter, I want to forgive him, I want to tell him I know, it doesn't matter, I'm sure he paid and paid for fucking that chicken – Longita had a passion for penance, she would have seen to that.

The mud clutches at my feet and legs. We're alongside the

channel now, a deep wide muddy trough. On the other side mangrove roots dangle above the mud, in the air, dainty verticals waiting for the tide. Everything is base and beautiful here. Everything is just what it is. I will not tell Nicky any of this. I can't explain how it is that moments of love come at me from the craziest places, escaping from the gaseous pockets in the sucking mud, from the slippery strata of what we've seen and cannot avoid. This skin. This knowledge.

# Woman on a Log Bridge

OKAY, SO HERE I AM, arms outstretched and halfway across this damned bridge, Mac. If you can call it that – two logs suspended above a creek. There's the pepper bush on the other side, see, and it's what I'm aiming for, eyes fast on the tiny flames, each pepper a different shade from its neighbour. God, what a country, to produce a bush like that, with no Moses to see visions in it or hear the voice of God, just me walking toward it on this log bridge, praying not to slip, not to go down with those tiny pepper flames shooting high and heavenward above me as I fall.

One log's stiff, Mac, like you. No resilience, no give. The other's swaying, springy, and so it's 'my' log, indecisive, up and down, a real bouncer. I look like a penguin crossing this thing, the weird shuffle, absorbing asymmetry with my knees, my hips. But hey, *I'm a man*, I can do this shit.

Just watch me.

The first day I came back here behind the ponds and saw this damned bridge, I knew I'd have to cross it, to show you, to prove it even though you're never going to know, never going to see. Miles away – where, in Brazil? Still? Having a gay old time of it? You didn't like Ecuador, they weren't nice to homosexuals. You couldn't cross-dress for fun here, not that you did it that often back home but God, you made a fine Marilyn. I've seen the pictures – so realistic, they made me queasy. It wasn't homophobia, was it? Tell me it wasn't. I lost sight of you in those pictures, the hair and make-up too convincing, beaming a drag-queen beauty, five by seven, high gloss.

I'm crossing this bridge, Mac, see? For you. And my heart

is going *bom, bom,* regular tympani, and all the blood in my body, God knows how many quarts, is at this moment pushing for a quick exit through my eardrums, *bom, bom, bom.* My head is huge and my neck is a spindle and my hands are lightweight, drunk, flapping east and west of my body marooned halfway across this bridge. My hips don't work, Mac. My legs are shaking. I can't breathe. This is all for you. Fuck you, anyway.

How about that other bridge, the one where all this started, in Papallacta, behind the public pools that were closed or too dirty, I don't remember why we didn't swim in them. Was it the weather? Sort of drizzly, a greasy kind of cold and you were hunting for orchids again and usually it was so good with you, Mac, such fun, so innocent. Like when we'd sing all the songs from *Funny Girl* in the backs of buses, or on roadsides with our thumbs out, you speaking the Spanish for both of us when a car stopped, or when we had to tell the bus driver how far and not letting people charge us too much because we were blond. Ya, Mac, how about that other bridge, the rushing water and the rocks below and no other way to get across, no going around except if we went all the way back to the road, which you'd never've been willing to do and which I'd have been too ashamed to ask.

You walked over that bridge without thinking, all boyish saunter, and when you got to the other side you stopped and turned, waiting for me to do the same. I couldn't. Your eyes said everything that you didn't need to put into words – what a wimp, what a baby, how tired you were of playing daddy and taking care of me. I WAS AFRAID, and you were disgusted with me and we were on either side of a log bridge in the Andes and I didn't know how to say I'd been raised to carry fear with me like a lump in my pocket that showed and never let me be streamlined or serene, and it would weigh me down on one side and make me fall. And then it would hold me down and make me drown in the cold rushing runoff from the Andean snowfields. Your face said it all and you waited and then you slowly came partway across and I moved toward you and was a third of the way out and then you were shouting at me, 'What's wrong with you!' in a voice without affection or restraint, the kind of voice you hear people using with family when they think no one's listening, the cornered-animal voice. You were shouting, 'I can't go backwards.'

So I did. I backed towards the bank again and then we started over and you know, I know we got across in one try but I don't remember how. For the rest of the afternoon there was something sour and terse in your replies: 'Unh-hunh,' or 'I'll think about it,' and then just plain 'No,' three times, until I took the hint and stopped making conversation. We didn't sing any songs between rides on the way home. In my mind the shape of that day is the taste of fear in my throat and the grey weight of your disappointment.

So that's what this particular bridge is all about, Mac, and no one's here to help me and I'm fine. Oh ya, I'm scared as shit but I'm here, halfway across, and if I fall it's only me to help me scramble up slippery banks with whatever sprain or break I earn from one misstep, which, by the way, isn't going to happen. I've got those hot little peppers cheering me on and the sun above me shucking sweat down my back and riveting my head to my neck to my spine to my legs. The sun is glue and it's holding me fast to these bleached logs halfway across this gully.

You should see me now, Mac. Not that it would make a whit of difference; I'm still in Ecuador and you had learned to hate it by the time you left whereas I took it all to heart, I mean I took Ecuador to heart and I took you to heart, too. It's like you're in there, tucked away in some valve with the *bom, bom* of my blood pumping past.

And in this little picture I carry, this love locket inside my chest, a small scene plays and replays itself: it's you and I on a log bridge in the mountains of Ecuador. The day is grey and our hair is blond against a leaden sky. I'm moving towards you and you're moving towards me, but everything in your face is wrong, and the sound inside that love locket is always the same. It's the sound of rushing water and a man shouting like a boy, 'I can't go backwards. I can't go back.'

# One in Every Port

FOR A WHILE she managed to juggle them, a man on the coast, another in the capital, that sprawling city climbing up the slopes of a grey-green mountain. It wasn't necessarily the sexual freedom she required, although she liked it, liked the difference between bodies, beds and styles. It wasn't even the challenge in it, of keeping the two separate and each, for the most part, unaware of the other's connection to her. Magda realized that her need to be with two men was a direct result of her need to be two women, two distinct selves. Magda *uno* and Magda *dos*.

She's been here a long time. Can't think a straight sentence in English any more.

Magda walks to the side of the balcony and places her hands on the wood rim of the half-wall. It's a nightly ritual, looking out to sea one last time before going to bed. When Carlos is here he joins her, but this morning he went upriver and so she's on her own tonight, grateful for the peace and solitude. She savours the moment, feeling sleepiness like a weighted cloak around her shoulders. The tide is going out. At some point in the wee hours it will turn and build toward a high tide at dawn.

Behind her, a hurricane lamp by the door throws a circle of light beyond the balcony walls. The night air is black and gold, particulate with pollen and small whirring insects. Something swoops into the shadow cast by her body, then veers off. Startled, Magda lets out a tiny yelp.

'Silly,' she says softly, 'it's just a bat,' and then bites her lip to refrain from continuing out loud.

Not that anyone will hear her if she does, but that's

precisely the point. A woman alone on the beach is cause enough for speculation. If she becomes too accepting of these behaviours in private, if she loses her self-consciousness, the next step will be public displays of weirdness, talking to herself on the street, picking at her cleavage or rubbing up against posts like a cat in heat.

She's felt fragile about her position here, in the community, ever since she moved north on the beach and into this house, when it was obvious there was no going back to Shane. That was a year ago. For more than half that time she's been connected, in people's minds, with Carlito, whom everyone adores. But they're not married and though he's asked her to move in with him, they still maintain separate residences. She tells him she needs her solitude. It's not a lie. As an artist, she does require time alone, but the whole truth is a little more complicated.

Up in the city, she sees Robert, as urbane as Carlos is sweet, as sophisticated as Carlos is fun-loving. One in every port, that's her motto now. A kind of survival technique, she reasons. Her justification for this, for the 'balancing act', is what happened with Shane.

Shane. At the beginning, it was that kind of relationship, the kind that changes you, that makes you willing and eager for change. She thought she was malleable enough, she thought she'd died and gone to heaven when he asked her to live with him on the coast. He was adventure and risk and being with him made her feel like everything could be different. She knew he'd been through a lot. A man with a past. She was falling in love all the way down the mountain, her belongings in one large suitcase on the top of the bus. But the reality of living with Shane was more than she'd bargained for.

It wasn't that the relationship went sour, she thinks, but that Shane changed. Or maybe just showed his true colours. A black-and-blue flag. She suspected Korea was the cause of the wicked rage inside him. The long-ago but, for Shane, still horribly present scenes of devastation and death. Routing screaming kids and old people from a burning village, bodies heaped up and stinking in the heat, bloating in decay. Sometimes Shane thrashed around in his sleep, yelled words she didn't understand, whimpered and curled into a little ball, the sheets tortured into a damp topography beneath their bodies.

Drinking, he told half stories sometimes, shards of memory piercing him, working their way to the surface. It usually meant he wouldn't go to bed until he passed out. And then it meant Magda might be woken near dawn by the weight of his sweaty body, hands gripping her shoulders till they hurt, his tongue huge in her mouth and his penis, first forcing and then ramming away inside of her. She knew better than to stop him. She'd read somewhere about the danger point in sleep. Dream rape, she decided, was preferable to dream murder. He seemed to remember little of this the next morning, or if he did, refused to explain.

And then one day he started drinking at lunch and by four he was pushing her around and calling her a cunt and then he was trying to break one of her long legs over the wooden bedstead of the bed they'd shared already for six months. She'd screamed at him to stop and something, she's not sure what, maybe the plaintive howling of the dog outside the bedroom door, had penetrated the fog of rage. He let go of her leg. Suddenly he looked stupid, stunned. He muttered, 'You better leave,' and walked out of the room. She scrambled off the bed and locked the door behind him. In fifteen minutes she was packed. She'd limped to the beach, thankful that it was low tide; there'd be a certain amount of traffic north to town. She'd flagged down the first truck that passed. Beyond that she remembers none of the details of the journey from coast to mountain.

In the capital she walked around in a daze for two weeks. The doctor she'd gone to had looked at her sharply over his glasses when she'd lifted her long skirt to reveal the blue and purple bruises on her thigh.

Even now, a year afterward, it's still a shock. She finds it hard to think of herself as an abused woman but the pain was real and made worse by shame and the horror of experiencing herself in a situation she had only imagined could happen to other women, not her, not this brave, independent self she had created. She'd found this little house right away and moved her stuff out of Shane's. But she jumped at every little sound and burst into tears at the smallest things, a bottle of spilled ink, a paper cut, a tiny worm wriggling through the cheese she'd just bought at the *tienda*.

The nights were worse. Sometimes she didn't fall asleep until three or four in the morning, hearing the wind in the palm trees or a rat on the roof. And then when she did sleep, she had bad dreams. They weren't specifically about Shane; she often couldn't remember anything about them except the way they woke her up, heart pounding, her T-shirt glued to her chest.

She was becoming the kind of woman she'd vowed never to be, fearful, timid. 'Get busy,' she chided herself, but it wasn't enough to work at her painting all day, alone with her thoughts. 'Get out of the house.' And stop talking to yourself all the time, she added, silently.

It wasn't difficult to persuade the local school to give her a job teaching English. She went into town three afternoons a week, working diligently through the basics of numbers and colours and how-are-yous, though many of the boys fished all night with their fathers and often fell asleep at their desks.

Friends, Darlene and Ray, owned a shrimp farm across the river. She started going there more frequently and up to

Quito once a month. And over time, the city offered her a distraction.

Robert was a well-travelled Brit; he'd worked in tea in India and come to South America because 'it was infinitely preferable to going home.'

She suspects he couldn't go home now, except perhaps to retire. He'd been an expatriate for half his life and liked the role of privileged outsider too much; his stories rolled out seamlessly. Short, bald and very charming, he had a flair for understatement, for mild self-deprecation. He'd ridden elephants, hunted tigers, collected beetles 'big as a fist', and at the urging of a native guide, eaten their larvae on jungle treks. 'A cross between chicken and pears, I'd venture. Quite satisfactory.'

For Magda, he was the perfect no-strings-attached man. Never again, she'd vowed when she left Shane, would she allow one man to mean so much.

Robert liked good food and drink, he liked to have an attractive intelligent woman sitting on the other side of a white linen tablecloth. He liked knowing where they were going after the meal. It stroked his ego that the waiters, the maître d' and the other couples in the restaurant knew too.

Fucking starts in the mind, he told Magda after they'd become a kind-of couple, after people started looking over her shoulder to ask, 'Where's Robert?' when she walked into the bar alone.

Talk is foreplay, he told her. But Magda could not have cared less about talk. She needed him as the next step, a new series of days and nights to erase and replace what her body remembered of Shane. She was accruing touch in layers, she was letting her body forget, not just the beatings but the way she'd needed Shane, physically, the way pity and love and something else, something she couldn't name or pin down, had drawn her to him in the first place and kept her there long past the time common sense told her to get out.

This was the antidote. Sex with Robert was teaching her body a language it had temporarily forgotten.

Through Darlene and Ray she met Carlos. A Colombian, he'd just bought property in the area and, with a crew of locals, had started the muddy work of carving ponds out of the mangrove.

She wasn't going to sleep with him, at first. She wasn't going to complicate her life. But he was spending a lot of time at Darlene and Ray's. It was where she'd go when the cabin fever took over, too many nights alone in a row. She usually took a bottle of rum and stayed overnight. Lately, so did Carlito.

The first few times they were there together, she headed off to bed in the small room next to Darlene and Ray's, leaving him the room off the kitchen.

One night, as usual, they were all sitting around the kitchen table. Ray had gone out to the porch and down the steps to pee in the yard. Carlito was pouring another round. A bit off-key, Magda and Darlene were singing along to Fleetwood Mac.

'Whoa oa and a landslide bring me down.'

Carlito winked as he handed her the drink, *'Cantas como una angelita*. You sing like an angel.'

'We sound awful!' Darlene laughed in response, looking at Carlito looking at Magda. She'd suddenly made a show of yawning and stretching. Ray walked back into the kitchen and reached for his drink.

'Last one, honey,' said Darlene cheerfully. As Ray began to protest she dug him in the side with her elbow. Under her breath, she said, in English 'The lovebirds need to be alone.'

It was a cane house, so the structure shook a little as Darlene and Ray climbed the staircase to the second floor. From upstairs she called out, 'I'm just going to pop another tape in for you guys.' The speakers crackled and there was the high whistle that signalled the start of the music. It was a slow, jazzy number by Chet Baker. Carlito stood by the table holding his hand out to Magda and then she was in his arms and dancing, the decision made before she let herself think about it. And at some point during the dancing he brought his hand up to her face and gently held her chin. She looked into his eyes and in that moment thought, 'I'll have to tell him,' but he leaned into her mouth and kissed away the words before they had a chance to form.

Later, she reasoned he didn't want to hear – or know – anything that might prevent them from being together.

'It's not like men haven't been doing this to women for ages,' said Darlene. They were standing at the wooden counter finishing the breakfast dishes. Magda was washing, Darlene was dipping the soapy dishes in a bucket of rinse water and then placing them on the small cane shelves and racks overhead where they'd drip-dry in minutes. Behind them, on the large cement *orno* in the middle of the room, dog food was cooking. Shrimp heads and oatmeal bubbled in a large aluminum pot. From its perch above the back of the benches surrounding the long kitchen table a parrot squawked, 'Corey, corey, corey.'

'Stupid bird,' Darlene responded, 'I've been trying to teach her "Ray" or "Darlene" for weeks. Who the hell is Corey?'

'He's such a nice man – no, not Corey, Carlito!' She laughed at Darlene's raised eyebrows. 'It feels a little deceitful,' she whispered, even though Ray and Carlito had already headed down the hill to the ponds and could be seen out of the kitchen window, walking along the dikes, Ray pointing at something beneath the surface of the water, Carlito coming to a stop beside him.

'The thing is, you want them both,' Darlene said,

[ 87 ]

grinning, and Magda, though a little sheepish, had to admit she did. And not just want, need, because it occurred to her that this was more than mere selfishness.

It was the way to stay clear.

Sometimes it felt a bit schizophrenic, bouncing from one man to another, even though geography separated them and lessened the need for deceit. With Robert there was some justification. He dropped hints about his extracurricular activities; he seemed to assume that she had hers. She counteracted the jealousy she felt around him with thoughts of her relationship on the coast. When guilt toward Carlos crept in, she felt herself divide. While one Magda worried, the other responded with reassurance, or some matter-of-fact appraisal.

She's lucky to have figured this out, the neat logic of it: Magda *uno*, Magda *dos*.

'Mmm, bed,' Magda murmurs, taking leave of the sea and the yard, the fireflies winking from the palms. She walks back into the main room and closes the solid wood door, manoeuvring the rusty lock through the two metal loops. A stubborn old thing, it has to be squeezed shut with both hands. A turn of the wick snuffs one of the lamps and produces the quick stink of kerosene. She pulls down the mosquito net, tucking it carefully around the foam mattress on three sides. After climbing in she starts the fourth side. Halfway up she pauses and reaches out to the table to crank the key on the other lamp. The room is in darkness now; there's not much of a moon. She waits for her eyes to adjust so she can finish.

A part of her has drifted up to the ceiling. It isn't the first time. Maybe her two selves need an overseer, a third Magda to hold the others together. This silent self watches: Magda painting; Magda running on the beach; Magda making love to Carlos; Magda making love to Robert. Never mind.

She watches the long arm attached to the long shape under the cool sheet, the quick regular tugs at the aqua netting, looming toward the roof in a dark room. Magda closes her eyes, settles her head on the pillow and falls asleep.

———

Carlos is fiddling with the straps on his suitcase, his back to Magda. She knows he's upset to be leaving her, to be going home to Colombia for his brother's funeral. Dead at twenty-three. There's no phone in the village; from a neighbouring town someone brought the telegram yesterday, its contents minimal. 'Ernesto killed. Car accident. Come home.' They'll postpone the funeral until Carlos arrives, two or three days from now. Somewhere along the way he'll call his mother, he's desperate to know more.

People in the village have been wonderful so far. A loan for his plane ticket. The offer of rides and support. It helped yesterday, Magda realizes, that there were so many details to attend to, the practical minutiae of preparing for a journey, holding shock at bay. It gave them both something to focus on.

But last night, in her arms, he was shaking like a child with flu. It is possible that she slept for short periods. She doubts whether Carlos did at all. Both of them were up at the first glimmer of dawn. She made a pot of strong coffee and cooked a large breakfast which she knew neither of them would eat, just to have something to do.

Since the telegram he's been anxious, disoriented. Magda is aware of an uncomfortable flatness in her own response. Twice this morning she's caught herself daydreaming about Robert and is appalled at her own insensitivity, the automatic rerouting of attention to her own pleasure.

With one ear cocked for the sound of the truck, she places her arm around his shoulders.

[ 89 ]

'Should I go upriver while you're gone?' meaning to the land that has been cleared for the shrimp farm.

He is blank for a moment, then the question seems to focus him and he responds like the Carlos she's used to, '*No, mi amor*, you mustn't worry about it. The men will be there. They'll try to get some more done while I'm gone. You are so concerned for my *camaronera*. But you have your show to prepare for,' he means the exhibition she will have in Quito, a month and a half from now. Yet the pang of guilt she feels is real. Only in Carlito's mind is Magda this gentle and generous creature, a reflection of himself.

The truth is, she doesn't want to go. She'd be tolerated but not really welcome. The work would continue for a time and then there would be an invented crisis, perhaps even a real delay – so many already, she's been amazed at Carlito's equanimity. The foreman would describe it to her in elaborate detail, as if her opinion mattered. The convention of respect for her as the *patrona* would be upheld as long as she was in the vicinity. But behind it would be the firm and uncrossable boundary. She cannot negotiate on behalf of Carlos; she is not a Latina. She is not his wife.

With Carlos gone, the work will stop.

When the truck drives up, beeping, she actually sighs with relief. But her good man doesn't hear, he is heading down the ladder with his suitcase. She follows down to its base and across the yard. At the gate, she lays a hand on his arm.

'Carlos, *amor, cuidate*, you know I'll be thinking of you. Please tell your mother I am so sorry for her loss.'

Carlos envelops her in a brief firm hug, throws his suitcase up into the back of the truck and climbs into the cab alongside the one they call Cholo, who lifts a sweat-stained cap to Magda. The truck backs up the way it has come, just past the turn-off to the beach, the stink of diesel drifting back to her. From behind a grimy windshield, Carlos blows her a last kiss.

By the weekend Magda finds she misses Carlos more than she expected. He might have called when he got to the capital or from the border, just to send his love. It's the sort of thing he'd do. He'd have to dictate his message to the IETEL operator in the next town. She'd give it to someone going down to the dock, who would hand it to a fishermen going to Cojimies, who would stuff it in his shirt pocket to protect it from the salt spray and wind and then hand it to a boy on the beach, maybe the same boy that had just helped him haul the bow of his boat up onto the sand. And the youth would run it up to Señora Rocio's *tienda* where it would be opened and read by both the Sra and her husband – because who knows, it might be *urgente*, in which case the messenger, hardly tired and hopeful of a gringa's tip, would be asked to run it right over to Magda's house. But if it was just a note of *cariño* between a man and his woman, it would be folded carefully and folded again, and placed under the live turtle that doubles as a paper weight. And it would stay there, although perhaps alluded to in conversation with a tap, a nudge, a sly grin between the *señora* and one of her customers, until Magda herself walked into the shop to buy cheese or batteries, soap or toilet paper.

The tide's coming up. Darlene might have sent in a worker to buy groceries, or come in herself to see if her friend wants to go over for a visit. Magda wouldn't mind.

She's dreamt every night about Carlos and regrets that she wasn't softer, somehow, at his departure. He's such a good man, why does she appreciate this more in his absence?

Mind you, if she'd accompanied Carlos to the capital, would she have called Robert? She winces, knowing the answer: Magda *uno*, Magda *dos*. I really do love Carlos, she thinks. Yet with Robert she's connected to a sophisticated world, good food, fine wine, clever conversation. And a small bomb goes off in her belly when he walks into a room. Is that love? They've never said the word.

Something to talk about with Darlene, 'cause it'll be girls only; Ray's away in the States. She'll take a bottle of rum and stay overnight. Already she's relaxing into the mood of the evening ahead.

Magda is partway into town when she sees the blond woman coming towards her on the road. She doesn't recognize her at first, instead finds herself reciting an automatic inventory: tall, not as tall as me – wow, is she white, hasn't been here more than a day – that hair would make me sweat – pretty dress, but she could lose a pound or two. *Alison?*

'Alison!' Magda calls out and jogs to close the gap between them. She stops in front of the pale woman, sees the sweat beading on her lip. 'Hot, isn't it? Wow, what a treat, Darlene said you might be coming one of these days, how long are you staying? Did you just arrive? How did you come down? Oh, God, you can tell I haven't spoken English in a week. Well, teaching – but that doesn't quite cut it. Sorry! Hi! I'm not letting you get a word in.'

She gives her a hug, steps back expectantly, is shocked to see tears.

'Oh my gosh, what's wrong? Has something happened? Is Darlene, is Ray ... has someone been hurt?! Tell me!'

'No Magda, I'm, ah ... it isn't anything, I had kind of a tough trip down, oh look at me, I'm sure I look a sight, sorry, I'm not ... it's just that, oh ...' she trails off, wet eyes sliding away from Magda's. 'Have you got a Kleenex?'

'Not on me, but look, we can go back to my house for a minute, have a cup of tea or some *agua de coco*. There's still a lot of tide, I was planning to go across to the farm, have you been there yet or did you just get here this afternoon? If Darlene's in town ... do you know? Or did she send someone in?' Magda laughs a little, 'See, I'm doing it again,' she taps her head. 'Twenty questions. Cabin fever.' Magda is feeling inordinately pleased with this turn of events. Visitors are rare here – what a treat.

Briefly, she puts her arm around Alison's shoulders, the gesture reminding her of Carlos's departure. That's twice in one week, she thinks, I hope I do better this time.

Alison hasn't really looked at Magda yet. Shy, Magda thinks, continuing the mental appraisal. That naïveté, like those young Peace Corps do-gooders, but she didn't come with them, did she? American School, teaches math and science; yes, that's it. And this must be her first time to the coast.

Robert had bought Alison a drink some weeks back, during one of Magda's trips up from the coast. The younger woman had blushed and spluttered in the face of Robert's charm.

Later, in bed, he'd been offhand, even cruel in his remarks, 'If she wants to stay in this country she'll have to learn a few social graces, she can't expect people to take care of her.'

Oil and water, Magda thought. 'But, Robert,' she'd started, on the verge of defending her new friend. 'But- Robert what?' he'd countered and then held a finger to her lips as his arm encircled her waist. 'Let's leave,' he'd said, between kisses, 'the subject,' another kiss, this one longer than the last, 'of Alison,' he pronounced the name in a breathy falsetto, 'alone.' And Magda, squirming deliciously in the big bed, had been more than willing to comply.

The thought of her lover makes her stomach contract.

At the house, Magda has Alison stand under the balcony while she gets the ladder from the *bodega* and raises it into position. 'You go on up,' she says, tossing her the keys to the padlock. Alison misses the catch.

Spaz, thinks Magda and then is instantly remorseful. She strides across the parched grass and picks up the key chain where it landed.

'Sorry,' she says handing it over, 'bad throw,' though she

knows it wasn't. 'Go up and lie down, I'll get us a *coco*.'

Magda crosses over to the grove of low palms and enters the cool shade under the wide fronds. She spots a ripe coconut, twists it off the tree and then carries it, slung in her cotton skirt, across the yard and up to the kitchen.

She opens and drains the *coco*, then splits it down the middle. 'There,' she announces, half of a green globe filling each palm. 'Do you want meat or just *agua*?'

Alison sits up on the bed and looks out at Magda through the open door. She doesn't understand the offer. Seeing her confusion, Magda pushes both hands forward, and nods with her head toward the jug. Her third self is suddenly airborne. Observing.

'Oh. *Agua*, please.' In a quavering voice.

Magda steps into the house from the balcony to hand her guest the glass. In the dim indoor light, she can see tears sparkling on Alison's lashes. The hair on Magda's neck prickles. Her nostrils fill with the scent of apple shampoo and something sharper, fear?

She doesn't want to know this, does she, but she is a good girl, when she's not deceiving her men, and a good hostess, in spite of the humble appurtenances of her home. She pushes aside the melodramatic warning. She asks, 'Is there something else?'

'I, oh...' Alison's eyes have filled with tears, 'I came down, umm, here, to tell you something.'

'Well, tell me!' Magda hears the frustration in her own voice. Immediately squelches it. 'Tell me,' she continues in a cajoling tone, sitting down on the bed beside Alison. 'You seem so, oh I dunno, wrought up, sad, about something. What is it?'

'I just don't know how to start.' Saying this, she casts a sideways glance at Magda from behind the thick hair.

The shampoo smell is cloying.

'Tell me,' she says again.

'Robert.'

'Robert, what?'

But she's only pretending she doesn't get it. Magda stands and walks back toward the door to lean against the frame. This way she can keep one eye on the sea, on the calming, even repetitions of surf. 'How long has this been going on?'

'Two months.'

Magda's calculation is immediate. 'But I was just there last month! The two of you acted like you didn't know each other.' She can feel the blood rising to her cheeks, throbbing at her temples.

'I know,' Alison is looking down at her lap. 'We ... I didn't know it would happen so fast. It was all very, umm, new ... then. And Robert felt it was best not to tell ... yet.'

At each pause, Alison breathes as if unable to fill her lungs. The sound of the shallow rasps, even more than the words, is almost more than Magda can bear.

'But I was sure you'd guess. I mean I was so, oh ... just so *nervous* when we went out that night.' She appeals to Magda with her eyes.

'Well, Alison,' Magda replies, her voice deep and level, 'I didn't think your nervousness meant you were sleeping with my boyfriend.'

'But he's not your boyfriend any more, Magda, don't you see, can't you tell? We've fallen in love. And we're going to be married. He's going to come home with me after school is finished, to meet my parents. We've talked about children already. I think he's made to be a father, don't you?'

Magda finds herself contemplating a hitherto unimaginable prospect. Robert? A dad? She can't picture it. Robert with his tiffin, or pippin or whatever the hell it is, high or low tea. Drinks at sundown. Weekend lie-ins. The towels that warm his cheeks in the ritual of the morning shave. She imagines his ordered British world with toys and diapers strewn about, a flustered Robert wiping spit-up from the collar of his lightly starched shirt.

The image is funny for a nanosecond. Hire a nanny, she's about to say, preferably one with a valet-husband. But tears of anger swell in her throat. God damn you, she's thinking. Why am I even thinking about this? How is this happening?

Alison, having found her tongue, is unstoppable. 'I know you want what's best for him. I just know it. If you could just see how we are together, you'd understand. And anyway, it's not like you and Robert were, well, really a couple. I mean, all those other women,' she throws a look at Magda, as if to say, 'aren't men exasperating?'

'He's not going to do that any more. They were really just for, well ... sex. It's the way it is here, he explained it to me.' Oh Christ, thinks Magda.

'Ecuadorian women really go for foreigners,' Alison babbles on, 'they think it's a ticket out to the States or Europe, you know, a chance at a more comfortable life. And I can't really blame him, when women throw themselves at you, and men, oh you know, they need it in a way that we, well, we just don't ... do we?'

Magda is glued to the door frame, gazing out at the ocean, the curls of white that form and skate along the tops of incoming rollers, the crash and foam as tide meets beach. She has a sudden desire to be in the water, swimming out through big waves. For a moment the thought is transporting, and she's free of the hot room and the oppressive conversation.

'And he wasn't in love yet.' Alison has picked up where she left off, but in a slightly subdued voice. 'I was mostly worried about you because you and I are starting to be friends.' She pauses, waiting for confirmation.

Magda says nothing. Hopes her own thundering heart cannot be heard.

Alison resumes with fake cheeriness, a trouper of an actor in a bad play where no one else seems to have memorized their lines, 'I told him, "Robert," I said, "let me talk to her, woman to woman." I wanted to. He didn't agree at first but I asked him, I said, "Robert please," and he really is so sensitive, I knew he'd see it my way. I knew you would too.

'I mean, the two of you weren't planning to stay together. You have another, well, life down here.' She emphasizes the word 'life'. 'Carlos, isn't that his name?'

Magda feels a kind of spasm in her gut. How dare she?

But Alison isn't finished yet. 'When we started, Robert and I, well, at first I felt badly. But he said, no, that it was kind of like old friends between the two of you and had been for some time.'

'Old friends.' Magda echoes these last two words softly, seeing the words as a kind of silent movie caption under the last time she and Robert shared his bed.

There's a sound from the yard below. Magda walks across the open kitchen, looks over the wall and into the eyes of a grinning youth below.

'*La señora Darlene dice que venga a Chuleta's para tomar cervezas.*' He winks, he raises his hands, palms up, in the universal gesture meaning, 'what next?' which here, now, means C'mon, *Señorita* Maggie, give me some *sucres*, I've come all the way from town and the *Señora* Darlene has already paid me for the trip but you're a gringa and maybe you're good for a tip too.

Magda doesn't give the boy an argument. Instead, relieved at the distraction, she flashes him a wry grin and tosses down a wrinkled ten-sucre note. How straightforward is the exchange of charm for money. Even when she complains about the culture and feels restricted by its rules, she sees its logic, and can take comfort in some of its habits.

It occurs to her, now, that if Robert had been 'stolen' by a

Latina, there'd have been a way to wrap her brain around it. A way to say to herself, I was stupid. I left him alone too long and this is what happened. But Alison is a gringa, and so the betrayal is deeper, wider than Magda could have imagined and even the luxury of pain and recrimination must be put on hold. Alison is still convinced of her good-buddy mission down here, and they are trapped in their combined allegiance to the farce of North American politeness – no brawling allowed, no cat fights, no satisfaction in the foreseeable future of the urge to punch that plump flesh and yank that apple-stinking hair. There are still the next few hours to be got through before Magda can foist her uninvited, unwanted visitor off on Darlene for the night and return here with her confused feelings, wondering if she even has the right to cry.

She needs a drink. Preferably now, and in vast quantities, even intravenously. 'All the better for a quick trip to blotto,' as Robert would say.

As Robert *would* say, God damn him!

Alison stands sheepishly at the top of the ladder, while Magda closes and bolts the door.

'Go on down,' she tells her. Is the woman a complete imbecile?

The boy is still waiting in the yard, probably because a walk to town with two gringas verges on heavy entertainment in these parts. From above, Magda watches his eyes on Alison and, not caring if the young woman understands, says, 'Look all you want, but those *tetas* are spoken for.' Is that what Robert sees in you, she wonders? Big tits and an air of innocence, something to quell the panic of his mid-life crisis.

'Oh, God,' she thinks, 'I need a beer.'

––––––––––

She sees the white envelope, the familiar handwriting, peeking out from beneath the turtle, the moment she walks into the *tienda*. Six weeks, she thinks. Not even a telegram to send his love. Grief, she has said to herself. Grief, she's explained to Darlene.

And with every passing day, she's been hoping for the sound of his whistle from the yard below, or the sight of his kind face and broad brown shoulders over the half wall of the house, greeting her with a wave as she comes up the beach after a run. Lately, before falling asleep, she has played a game of prediction and hope, dividing his route back to her into stages. Each night she has imagined him starting and completing a single increment of the journey: Carlito in Bogota, getting on a plane; arriving in the capital and taking a taxi to a friend's to stay overnight; boarding an early bus and descending the mountain; pulling in to the noisy port city and, yes, getting a room, because it's late when he arrives and the buses along the coast have stopped for the night. He's eating in an open-air café, fried fish and *platano* and a couple of beers to wash it down. He's striking up a conversation with the man at the next table and buying him a beer – he's that kind of person.

And in the morning, after a *café tinto* at another sidewalk restaurant he boards a bus going south. He looks out of the open sides of the bus at the palm trees and cane houses and waves at little kids in dirt yards. In Muisne, he goes directly to the wharf. He hops into a boat, within minutes it's speeding through channels bordered with the dangling roots of *manglar*. He's joking with the fellow at the tiller, accepting his condolences – joy and pain, the Latino ease in their combination. Now they're racing full out across the open stretch of river facing Cojimies, getting closer and closer still, almost here, almost, and then they are, the engine is cut, the boat bumps against firm sand. Young boys are running down the beach. Carlito is stepping out.

That's where she'd placed him last night, tempting fate.

She stares at the letter, still sealed, and knows the strength of her own imagination because it has arrived on the very day she has willed his journey to end and her long wait to be over. But why a letter, why not Carlito himself? She doesn't want to read it, not yet.

She pushes the letter deep into her skirt pocket, finishes her shopping, walks back through town, past the graveyard. Just before the whorehouse, a sweet rich scent assails her, something in bloom. She pauses, looking for the tree or bush, identifies what she thinks is the source, and watches herself walk to the tree, watches herself lean into it, inhaling. Casual, relaxed, a woman who stops to smell the flowers. Then she continues on down the dusty road to her own fence. She puts her *compras* away, biscuits and cheese in separate plastic containers and then in a hanging basket. Detergent in a bucket under the table. Toilet paper on a stick protruding from the cane wall of the bathroom. She busies herself with household chores until late in the day, cleaning and organizing the shelves where she keeps her clothing and books, leaping once when a large spider scuttles out from a dark corner. Shortly before sundown, she grabs a thin jacket, locks up, descends the ladder and heads toward the beach.

She walks north as the sun descends and the gold slanted light deepens to rose, bathing the sea and land. She walks past the beginning-to-rot smell of two small hammerheads and the tiny fish that the fishermen haven't bothered to clean or keep. About a mile from the house, she stops at a bleached log and sits, pulling the letter from her pocket. She tears along the one end and extracts the single sheet of airmail paper. It flutters and snaps in the offshore breeze.

She looks out at the red sun entering the ocean, stares at it a moment as if for courage, takes a deep breath and begins to read.

The letter is brief, its opening devoid of Carlito's usual

warmth. He writes, 'I am needed here. I will not be back for some months.' His mother, he explains, cannot manage the business on her own. The next line neither shocks nor surprises her. 'When I return, we cannot be together. Our cultures are too different.'

Someone, '*un amigo*', has informed him of her other 'situation'. 'I can only imagine that you needed something this man gave you. That somehow I was not enough.'

She stands up, folding the letter carefully. It pains her to recognize the truth in Carlito's words. He hadn't been 'enough'. She could write him begging his forgiveness, she could confess that she had been dropped by Robert like so much loose change, but she knows it won't salvage the relationship. He has the Latino sense of honour. Magda has betrayed him.

The skin of her cheeks tingles where tears fall and cool and dry. Hugging the thin material of the jacket around her arms, she looks out over the water. Only a faint greenish glow indicates where the sun has been swallowed by sea. Her eyes follow the horizon line, ocean and sky almost indistinguishable from each other in the gathering dark.

So it dissolves, her perfect system, Magda *uno*, Magda *dos*. For a moment, she wills that third Magda to take over, to float now above this sad self, or pull her mermaid-like into the dark and undulating sea. But her imagination cannot or will not comply.

'Just me now,' she says, for once not caring if she's overheard.

She starts back, bare feet slapping the firm, cool sand. Distant trees screen the village from view. Her own house is partially obscured, but she can make out a patch of its roof and the grove of coco palms beyond it. In a now indigo sky, the evening's first stars have appeared.

# Testosterone

THE ENGINES COUGH and bark in their stalls, like so many cranky beasts that need a drink of oil, each man/boy bringing his steed, his mount to a full pitched whine; you can't breathe for the stink of exhaust, can't think for the agony of sound that psychs everybody, racers and crew and fans, even you, not sure you want to be here, the racetrack at Yaguarcocha, Lake of Blood.

But you're annexed to your Texan boyfriend Russell and his best buddy Jake, and this is their passion. Motorcycle racing. In the pits the two tall gringos stick out above all the younger locals, through gas-ups, tinkerings, the eager encouragement and last-minute advice from the hangers-on too scared to ride. Tall heads bend to take it in.

Gassed up, zipped into leathers, a dozen men are crouched above snarling motors. And what's going on under those helmets, behind those windscreens, is anyone's guess: nervous or dead calm or that strange stasis before going at a ridiculous speed on something that, when stationary, falls over without a kickstand.

Machismo. The flag drops and swoops, signalling two things, the flagman's self-importance and the start of the race. A dozen bikes blow into the opening stretch, faster than you can do anything. Moments before, you'd said, 'Don't fall!' and he'd promised, 'I won't.' But the only other time you watched him race, he rode a dirt bike up a fence, hit a bystander and for a long awful moment you thought they were both dead.

You spend twenty laps praying and pacing the observation deck, spooked by its low cement walls and the parking lot four stories down. In Canada they'd have railings or it would be glassed in, safety first, but not here, not in Ecuador, where small wooden crosses dot the roadside and the bus drivers play chicken, patting the polychromed Virgins plastered to the dash. Christ, there isn't even an *ambulancia* on hand.

You're looking for the white numbers you cut and pasted carefully on his headlights, a four and a seven, his age; looking for his bulk; his dark colours. Twenty laps, you hold your breath, waiting for your man to make it safely round the circuit one more time. The motors scream by. It makes you think of migraines, though you've never had one, or cells imploding. Then you don't have to imagine; one boy crashes, flips like a doughnut or a dinner roll, light and fast and hopping off the track onto green swale, somersaulting slo-mo as if all the watching eyes are TV cameras, and finally comes to a rest. Sweet Jesus, is he dead? (No, but he will be in two months, riding helmetless on a downtown street. Cut off by a bus and slammed into a tree, he'll hang on for three days, comatose, while the racing community bring sheepish expressions and sympathy to his family, distraught in the hospital waiting room.)

Word snakes through the crowd; somewhere there are radios and officials, static, excited jabbering.

'He's moving.'

'He's shaky, but he's standing.' And even with the broken hand, the bruised ribs and the pulled tendon the kid gets back on and finishes the race – testosterone.

Testosterone. In the air so thick you can reach out and grab some, turn, temporarily, into a man. You're hyper, revving like an engine, gearing down and up through your fears, through the please-please of weak faith; so short-lived, it takes the sight of him, safe and steady each lap, to be renewed. Through all that you feel the small animal growl of competition in your belly, the horns of it sprouting from your forehead. Osmosis, you're as pumped as those fluid, focused men and boys down there, like the tigers in the story kids don't read any more, 'cause it ain't PC. But here, no such rules exist and so, like Little Black Sambo, you wait for the speeding bikes to turn to butter, to liquid lead, to mercury. Faster, faster.

Then, so suddenly, it's over. Jake, one of the middle-aged gringos, has won the race, skinnier and swifter than everyone here.

You had a fling once, more than a decade ago. You feel a fondness for him now that you hide from Russell; it's an odd feeling, tinged with embarrassment and exasperation. Sometimes Jake's vanity is tiresome, and for the most part, you don't approve of the way he treats his wife. But the men in this country style themselves on different heroes than you might select. He was always the Peter Fonda of the expats, known for his speed and his guts and his cool head, but years ago with your arms around him, he felt smaller than you, skin so soft between the moles and scars, a mapping of every crash he'd ever had, every guardrail he'd wrapped that lithe body around.

And maybe in a nod to all the miles he'd logged they took away three-quarters of his stomach and some of his looping intestines. But you think it was rpm and mph that eroded him, and never letting anybody hold him down that makes him now the skinny shadow of his former skinny self.

After the race he's crowing, they've got microphones and cameras in his face, and in Russell's too – he's number two – and you're just so glad to have them both back and standing still, you think, yeah, big sigh of relief, it's over. But fast and soon, you learn it's not.

First there's the awards ceremony, they'll film it for TV. And the prizes are beribboned in the colours of the Ecuadorian flag: thin stripes of yellow, red and blue. The cups have tiny gilt goddesses – pert breasts and thin wings – on little marble stands. And guess what, the men get to choose who's gonna hand it up to them, their prize, their token kiss on the platform. You hate this, you're supposed to be delighted to be basking in reflected glory and look cute too, big smile for the clapping crowd. I'm too old, you think, but hey, at a distance the tits and ass still check out.

Finally, it's time to go. It's decided where the two trucks will rendezvous for lunch and you think, good, I'm hungry, all morning on adrenalin and coffee and sips of beer. In the *Hacienda Whatsits*, the menu is great and the view is pretty but you don't know the rules and Jake's wife has already given you shit for not being enthusiastic enough on the platform.

The first fight is happening before you know it. On every peach tablecloth is a perfect rose. 'Blush,' you say, knowing the colour. Someone bumps your table and the rose suddenly teeters and falls. Water spreads on the cloth and Russell grabs the upended vase and he's using the big, beautiful rose as a mop and automatically you reach for it and say 'Oh no, don't do that,' and faster than he went around that track your man is swatting your hand, harder than he realizes, and the shock and pain race you backwards to the only other times in the past a man hit you.

A Toronto suburb. You were sixteen, seventeen maybe, and going up to a cottage with friends – one of whom was the boy you loved who had been trying, afternoons, after school, to get you to go all the way. Your dad stopped you in the doorway with, 'I can't ask you to be good, can I?' and as the words were spitting out, he'd grabbed an arm and pushed it like a lever, like you were an obstinate machine that wouldn't start, or that, starting, wouldn't run properly. He pushed you back into the house. But you ran to your mother, crying, 'You know what he just did?' and went anyway, the weekend a disappointment for your young and eager boyfriend, because the whole time you were away you felt the grip on your arm, keeping you guilty and good, shoulda stayed home.

The next incident was the next boyfriend, on his way out but not wanting to be and beside himself with frustration, a little drunk, who reached up and closed his fingers around your neck and shoved, not too hard, and then focused on his hand as if it were a separate entity, an animal that had somehow gotten off its leash. He dropped his arm then and tried staring an apology into your eyes but you'd already made up your mind, 'I'd never stay with a man who hits.' Saying it, you could taste the power, the delicious righteousness.

But you'd had options then, and youth, and now you're not so sure. Why here, why now? 'Never,' it's like a gong in your head, 'never, never,' an insistent echo. Dammit, who'd have thought this man would?

Well, everybody, that's who. He's a macho redneck with a temper, six motorcycles, a bit of a death wish and a drinking problem. Oh, not to mention the gun that is always only a grab away. He sleeps with it under his pillow. But I hate stereotypes, you think, as if the force of your personality and projections are gonna change a damn thing.

Russell is staring at you, and his eyes are bloodshot, which makes the irises shine a more brilliant blue. If it weren't for your confusion and his anger you could return his gaze, and enjoy it, because he's a handsome man, although he looks ten years older than his age, with receding silver hair and a beard that he lets grow bushy whenever he's out in the oilfield.

His forehead and cheeks are bisected by deep furrows and there's a network of fine wrinkles around each eye. He's got the *petrolero's* skin, dark and toughened by years of exposure, and to look at him clothed you'd think he was that way all over, but you know that the undersides of his large biceps are loose hammocks of flesh, as soft as that same place on your mother and almost blue-white in comparison with the sunleather of his chest and shoulders. It's one of the things you love about his body, that and the impossible length of his legs, the way he brings his feet up under yours in bed, spooning, and the inventive variation he brings to that position to make early-morning love.

But none of that is in your mind right now. You can't even look at him because you're not sure which hurts and shocks you more, the blow or that he's not apologizing.

He is, in fact, furious. Doesn't know what he's done, 'cause with guys like this, it's degree, and he was raised with cuffs to his head and slaps across the face, and he was forty-four the last time his dad beat him up and a swat is not a hit, see? But even besides that he's so post-race, he's so high on that hormone, he's sitting beside you, 220 pounds of speed and bravura. Not a clue, he's still on that bike or on that platform, getting his kiss, his cup.

Ah, but. It's hard to be the also-ran, second place, and in the amateur category yet. To make matters worse, the kids are in the bathroom with their mom, which makes *numero uno* himself, Jake, the sole audience for the tiff. And pride is why your guy can't back down.

Russell wants you Here, Now, a Good Girl, glorying in him. The rose was a mistake but he can't admit it, can't take back what he will not recognize as wrong.

'Don't get all weird,' he says, but it isn't conciliatory, it's a threat.

French tourists have seated themselves nearby on the veranda, two tables together, a large group. The bubble of their gaiety rises in the hot afternoon, bounces off the solid wall of tension at your table. One of them, a bald fellow, preens in his European excuse-for-a-swimsuit, hyphen of green beneath his sweating sunburnt stomach. He has no interest in other tables except as mirrors, but his girlfriend is curious. She's a plain Jane, skin pale as porridge. You notice the cotton scarf around her hair; it aims for casual chic and doesn't succeed.

A Frenchwoman without style? Impossible. So she's the Unfrench, but your relief at this temporary distraction dissolves under the harpoon of her stare. You flinch. It never fails, in every public place a shark is circling, sniffing out the fish with the hook through its mouth.

Which is what your big Texan orders, from the sweet waitress, catch of the day, *pescado frito*. When it comes, he slathers it with *salsa de tomate*, the Spanish euphemism for ketchup.

Catch-up. Like there's another finish line he has to cross with beer. He has speed-swallowed the first two and he wants two more while you want to die, curl up under the table, be anywhere-but-here. Since the hit, you've done and said nothing except squirm in your chair and swallow hard, but he won't let it go.

'Chill out!' Russell barks.

Inside your head is an eight-year-old's whimper – leave me alone – like being in trouble at the end of the day, your father coming through the door, your mother handing him the wooden spoon. Nothing but that small scared feeling and nowhere to go. But somehow, your mouth is open, and your voice, in its lowest register, the one you reserve for firmness, for feminist debate, comes out of its own accord.

'No.' You pause, and then, emboldened, that same voice says, '*You* chill.'

Jake shifts in his chair, clears his throat. You wait, then risk a look at Russell. He's averted his gaze.

And for that or any of a million other reasons, the ticking of the clock, the layers of time, the fact that somewhere in the world someone is breathing, or eating a plate of couscous, or snoring softly beneath a pale pink mosquito net, you let it go. And a woman in a field is sowing runner beans at the base of new corn plants, so that the growing vines will spiral up the stalks and put forth their small, flirtatious flowers, a red as sudden as a kiss next to the green and purple cobs. For that you let it go. Somewhere, a woman with a baby on her back is picking lice from an older child's head, someone else is sewing on a bone-coloured button, or calculating sales tax while chewing on a plastic pen, and surely a funny-but-dumb joke has just been told somewhere in the world and people are laughing, perhaps even wiping tears from their eyes. For these things, for your new, post-therapy belief in the benefits of denial and distraction, for sheer relief at being let off the hook of his anger – because, God, maybe everything is a projection, maybe all he was saying was 'Don't leave' – you put your rule aside. There. Stay put.

The Frenchman has been to his room to put on a white golf shirt, but he's opted not to cover his bottom half. His forehead is the colour of cooked lobster, the perfect compliment to the bulge of lime green Lycra between his legs. And it occurs to you that if, at that moment, they held a boyfriend contest, you couldn't predict who'd lose.

So what gives with the Unfrench, her grey/green appraising eyes. Stop *fucking staring*. You scream it silently into your hands, fiddling at the edge of the damp tablecloth. The Unfrench didn't see the swat but she knows, doesn't she, and her stare is the refusal to let it go, and the rule is still there, it won't budge. Only now it's broken, a contradiction in terms, like the cold heat of dry ice. Like the hole it burns in your heart.

A month later, there's another race. This time he does crash. You don't cry till you know he's all right, bloody knuckles and his initials torn from the back of the black jacket. The shiny helmet is scraped white in the place where his head met pavement. He'll wait too long to get an X-ray for the source of the limp, two bones fractured in his foot. It'll hurt, but he'll refuse the cast and be cranky for weeks. For now, he's standing tall, getting clapped on the back, he and his buddies manoeuvring the crumpled bike up a plank and into the back of his truck. He's shining with heroism, already shaping it into myth.

'Gearshift popped out. Went down instead of gearing up. Pilot error. My own damned fault.' He slid fifteen metres on Tarmac before surfing into tall grass, green-gone-gold in the rainless months.

He cuts a wide swath.

Once again you hear the blood pumping at your temples. Whether it's good or bad with him. Love leaping from skid marks and trampled grass. Love. Through the hole in your heart.

# Hatchetface

HATCHETFACE. She was short, like five-two or something, and dark-skinned. She tanned easily to a nut brown. Dark hair too. A hatchet-faced, raven-haired woman. I'm waxing poetic. At any rate, she didn't stand out in the environment, if you know what I mean, not like a dove among crows or a lily among … what, let's go for something short and dark. Pansies? And not exotic enough, either. I mean, there are flowers for instance, since I'm on the subject, bromeliads and the like, spiky tropical blooms, ugly and captivating at the same time, that you look at and think, jeez, how does it work? Why did Nature make it? No answer forthcoming but still, you can hardly stop staring at it.

Her feelings for me go back to when she found out about us, I mean, me and him; she said it hurt a lot, because, 'You're so blond,' she said, 'so pretty.' Well, it's all relative I guess. I mean, in Canada I'm not. But down there, a small village on the Ecuadorian coast, ya, blond was the red-hot ticket. Lots of variables according to culture and geography on 'pretty'. Nail it down in one corner of the world and lose sight of it somewhere else. An elusive concept. But Winona sure as hell found something pretty when she married him. Lord, was he gorgeous.

I'm justified, by the way, in using the past tense. Age and drugs took care of his beauty. Took it away a cell at a time. Which adds up over all those weeks and months and years on that hot coast. And he's fat now too. Looks go. Beliefs get stale. Love segues to habit, to disappointment. You wake up one morning and the sense of adventure that beckoned you here is long gone, hardly remembered except for nights when a visitor pulls it out of you and it rolls off your tongue like the rum you're drinking, but the next morning there's just your hangover, a too-bright sun beating on the shrimp-ponds, the sticky, stinking heat, and a sour taste in your mouth. It's the taste of nostalgia, of something that didn't deliver. The visitor goes back home and you're on your own again, melting into torpor. Endless tropical nights stretch out ahead, bug-filled wastelands to be endured somehow. The kerosene lamps go phht and ssss and the cassettes are old and a lot of them just don't play any more.

Winona's the only woman I ever had the pleasure of hating. I borrowed her husband for the briefest possible period. Long enough to have a leg up. Like a dog, pissing out a territory. Like a bitch in heat, consenting finally to the leader of the pack. Not even such a catch after all.

Winona talked about their sex life like it was some raving roller coaster of positions and potency. 'We did it down by the pump on the path. God, was it good,' she said, into her cups one evening, just the girls, 'cause Gary was up in the capital. Sure you did, Winona, with the fire ants crawling all over your half-tanned ass. Sounds pretty blissful to me.

'We made the house shake last night,' she'd say in town, to anyone who'd listen. Like a cane house doesn't shake when you sneeze or just walk across the floor. Give it a rest, Winona, everybody knows it's bull.

There's a phrase in Spanish, how does it go? At any rate, the translation is something like 'she put horns on him'. Meaning, he was the cuckold; the husband of an adulteress. Winona fucked her way through the varied terrain of the country, up and down mountains and into the jungle, along the coast, upriver and downriver, putting horns on her husband with a certain geographical panache, and maybe it was a cry for help and maybe it's what a hatchet-faced woman does when her own husband no longer turns to her in the dark and maybe, maybe, maybe. Maybe I was part of some weird balancing act on the part of Fate, a ye-too-shall-be-screwed contract that floats around in the ether, one of the great karmic clipboards in the sky. Fucking Gary was my way of evening the score. I was happy to fuck Gary 'cause his own wife screwed around on him so much. That was how I sold it to myself, at the time. I was happy to lean forward in the Boston whaler so that my round little butt showed from underneath my short blue shorts, leaning over the bow like I was so interested in the colour of the water or whether there were fish in the channel or just how shallow is it here, anyways. Pretty damned shallow.

Gary and I had one good night together. Sexy. Steamy. Sliding around in the sweat and musk of each other. The next day he sent me home with a *racime* of bananas. If you've seen pictures of the plantations, you know there are these big bunches hanging off the plant. Tiers of green fruit around a thick stem, like rows of fingers getting ready to catch something. And down there, in banana-land, they refer to the smaller bunches as hands, *manos*. Well, some of them were sure to rot before I'd get around to eating them. Maybe Gary wanted me to think of something sweet, to think of his *manos*, yes, touching me everywhere. Maybe he wanted me to remember what was unlikely to be repeated 'cause that was the last time Gary intended to stray. Guilt? Variety is not the spice of life? He just wasn't cut out for it, for sexual transgression.

Sometimes couples divide the roles and the rules between them. Here's your outlet, honey, here's mine. Gary was happiest when he was taking apart a motor, grease up to his yingyang. He couldn't help being beautiful, being the kind of man women want, panting, parading their pert little buns and breasts around in his line of sight, hoping to get a rise out of him. I watched other women try after me; I knew he wasn't biting. One good night was all Gary could give me. But Hatchetface and I went many rounds. What's a man sometimes except a lever between two women, unconsciously throwing his weight and influence into one corner and then the next.

Y'see, I told her. I know, like I'm a major-league *idiota* but we were drunk one night, me and Sandy and Winona. Sandy's the connection, right? First, she's my friend from back in Canada. That's why I'm here in this hot little backwater on the equator. She's Winona's friend too 'cause gringas stick together and sometimes you just wanna speak English. Sandy alternates between putting up with Winona and avoiding her. She's tired of fibbing to Winona, of having this secret on her.

'Okay, Sandy,' I say. 'I see your point.' She's giving me this look: You better.

'Okaaay,' I say, 'All right, already. We can tell her the next time we're there.'

'We?' Sandy's got on her teacher voice. I let myself be shamed, be swayed. I think, sure, why not, no sweat really, 'cause I know that Winona in one of her guiltier moments had more or less offered Gary to Sandy. I figure the fling's been flung, the affair was pretty short-lived, she'll understand. What a dolt.

Within a few weeks we're at the shrimp farm and Gary's away, up the coast buying larva. I'm psyched. Tonight's the night, I'll make a clean breast of it.

'Listen, Winona, it was booze, okay?' Only I'm looking at her face and 'okay' is not the word for that expression. 'We just got a little, you know, carried away.' Her hairline is moving strangely, like the skin is trying to separate from the scalp. Now she's looking over at Sandy but Sandy's not looking at either of us.

'Just the one time, Winona.' Ah, yes, very reassuring, see that vein pulsing at her temple, the thin line of her lips pressing together, those two spots of colour high on her cheeks.

Hatchetface asks a few questions, mostly to do with when but the what is there, larger than life, a furry beast pressing up against all of us. I dunno, is it really hot in here or is it just me?

The miracle is that when I finally say good night and go upstairs, I actually fall asleep. Winona stays up all night with Sandy and by morning I'm the *femme fatale* from hell and the golden princess all rolled into one. I'm hanging with metaphors, I'm reeking, stinking with symbolism. The other woman. Done her wrong. Her Gary does it once with someone else and she's the scorned wife, the heartbroken heroine, she's got story power in this one to outlast any and all of her infidelities. Sandy's acting all parsimonious and pure, like you-get-what-you-ask-for. I'm sheepish I guess but at least a little less hungover than the two of them, and better rested.

'What did you expect?' Sandy asks when I mutter something about the morning mood. And then, as if I might have forgotten, 'You slept with her husband.' I can actually see the emphasis she places on that last word. It's in capitals, drawn and shaded to look 3-D, a big word in comic-strip granite. It drops from the cartoon bubble beside her head and lands with a crash at our feet. I look down.

We're all acting out our parts.

Hatchetface gets a regular snit on about it, hates my guts. Sometimes, months after the fact, we'll have it out. Gary shakes his head at us, from a distance. He still sneaks a kiss or two with me when he can, but we both know it won't amount to a thing. I'm not drinking so much any more. I never had the stomach for it. But Winona's always saying, 'We create our own reality,' and she likes to alter the one she's in with whatever's handy. She and Gary go from the sweet, clear high of refined coke, down through the months and years into the gag-me stench of base, cooking on a wire screen. They can blow a whole weekend huddled around that screen.

At the end of that year, I leave. Four years later I return. In the interim, my dad has died from pancreatic cancer.

Between when we found out about my father's illness and when he was gone there wasn't any time to fix decades of not saying what we felt, or knowing, even. I got remorse to last me the rest of my days.

I'm back in Ecuador 'cause something in me needs something here, but I don't need trouble so I don't go to the coast, I don't revisit the scene of the crime. The crime, as it were, visits me.

Gary and Winona have driven up from the coast with a cooler full of shrimp. Sandy has walked over the hills from the little house she lives in now, since she got tired of the bugs and constant dirt of life ocean-side. There we are, the four of us, in the living room of the place I'm house-sitting, thirty minutes southeast of Quito.

We've boiled, shelled and eaten the shrimp and scarfed down the cheese and bread. The wine they brought is all gone, and Sandy's up for it all of a sudden, in a real party mode, so she says there's more wine at her house and she and Gary get in the Jeep to go and get it, which leaves me and Winona alone under the high wooden rafters of the adobe living room and I can't imagine how we're gonna get through the next twenty minutes or so.

She's still got wine in her glass though mine is empty. The room already looks hungover. There's a platter on the coffee table with four or five uneaten shrimp on it, the remains of a humongous pile; I swear, they brought half a pond. On the same dish are several squeezed and discarded *limones*, the small tropical fruit that's the colour of a lime but tastes like a lemon. I'm tapping my fingers at the side of my chair, staring into the fire, trying to remember a magic spell from my childhood that'll make me or Winona disappear, me to fanta-syland and her to some black hole, any black hole, in space.

A eucalyptus log is burning in the fireplace, but the smoke that surrounds us is from the cigarettes they've been smoking all evening: Camel plains. Shrimp juice, red wine and the odd whiff from my own armpits – no, I'm not relaxed – add to the layered perfume of the room. Finally, as a distinctive top note, the tang of banana vinegar.

A jar of *aji*, hot sauce, stands open among the drained glasses and crumpled napkins. They brought it with them, because every region in this country prepares it a different way and Gary likes the coastal stuff. It's kind of intoxicating, that smell, and it's doing that olfactory trick of erasing years in a flash. It hooks me by the nose and drags me down the mountain to a cluster of small villages around the mouth of a river emptying slow brown waters into the Pacific.

Where the heat was like a second skin.

The sun on my head and the breeze on my shoulders and the mud sometimes up to my knees, all of it, was the land and sky holding on to me, a tropical embrace, an infiltration. And when there was no breeze the air itself was thick with heat and moisture so that it felt more solid than air but not yet like water, and I loved it, invasive as it was, and it made me into the kind of woman who could do that, sleep with another woman's man, because not only had the heat gone to my head, it had gone to my heart and hands and all the other parts of me. It wasn't right, but I knew why; I had slept with Gary because the tropics had melted a reserve at my core, and because he was there when that happened. I slept with him, but what Gary really gave me had little to do with a hot night and his body.

Under a sun-blasted sky we had often crossed the *boca*, the wide mouth of the river delivering itself into the ocean, and life is occasionally that simple; there is nothing like a fast ride in an open boat, with the light chop making a vibrato beneath my thighs, and the wind in my sun-bleached hair and on my sun-toughened skin. And though it was, sometimes, someone else, it was often Gary behind me at the tiller, and in my memory he has become synonymous with that feeling of freedom.

Remembering that makes me feel naked here, in this high-ceilinged room with its smoke pall and the detritus of our feast and a woman whose husband I borrowed.

'We create our own reality,' Winona's saying.

Shit, I'm thinking, I'm not up for this.

'We design it, we alter it.' Too many *Omni* magazines, Winona, too many sci-fi paperbacks. I'm listening hard for the sound of the Jeep. She still has half a tumblerful of wine. She's tapping an unlit Camel on the coffee table in front of her.

'Airplanes fly ...'

'... only because we believe they do,' I finish her sentence 'cause it's a speech I've heard before. Her eyes narrow, she seems to be seeing me for the first time. Her gaze shifts to the drink in front of her. She reaches for the glass, almost slo-mo, raises it to her lips, takes a small sip, and then another. She puts the drink down, positioning it just so, as if she's illustrating a point.

'We create it. Our own reality.'

Meaning you've created me, Winona, at least the role I've played in your life. Meaning your stupid theory works both ways. C'mon, you guys, get back here. There's no sound from outside, no distant grumble of the Jeep's motor, of its chassis squeaking as it labours up the cobblestone road. Just the flick of her lighter and the sweet tobacco stink of the cigarette she points into the inch-high flame.

'What are they doing, picking the grapes?' I say. Even to my ears, this sounds flat and pitiful, the way small talk always does in a charged atmosphere.

'Sickness, injury, we bring it on ourselves.'

Oh, Winona. Why did I ever underestimate you?

She knows how my father died, that his illness was sudden and merciless but she doesn't know that he aged thirty years in less than two months and that, at the end, he looked like my grandfather, beaky and scrawny, a withered life, a wasted body.

'Like cancer, for example. It's something you do to yourself.'

I'm screaming at her, 'Fuck off, just fuck right off,' 'cause she's getting back at me through the only man I've got and I don't even have him any more, he's dead and it happened too fast and she's not just implying, she's saying he did it to himself, meaning he did it to us, meaning hurt is this thing we all carry around inside us and only get rid of by passing it on. Winona's gonna make me pay if it's the last thing she does.

Well, the weird thing is, by the time the other two come back I don't even hate Hatchetface any more. I'm screamed out, hated out, score's even, *punto*. That's the word for period, or end. It's the severed tie, it's the whisper of an angel in the mountains lifting off a terra cotta roof and heading for the sky. It's like, ya, Winona, maybe we create these shabby little lives, maybe we fuck around on each other trying to make up for the won't-get and can't-have. Go home. I'm sorry. Life sucks. Gary's turned out not to be such a hunk, after all. And wine is just the colour of this one night.

# *Despedida*

DANA REMEMBERS the stinging pink of Mercurochrome on the scraped knees and elbows of her childhood but here in Cojimies, Ecuador, the colour for wounds is purple.

They are tying knots in a nylon string around her ankle, a knot per man. There are only the four women here tonight; Dana, the two other gringas, Gaby and Shelley, and Maria Luisa whose husband owns this beach-side bar. *Cumbia* music is crackling out of a tape deck. A generator hums from inside a cane shed. It is Dana's *despedida*, a farewell party to end her year in this tiny coastal town just north of the equator. Beer bottles appear in a steady stream, leave sweat rings on the chipped white Formica tables and then are tossed, empty, into the plastic crates called *javas* at the far end of the bar's wooden deck.

The knots the men tie are meant to bind them in memory to her. She will forget most of them by name and none of them by face. She has slept with only one of them and didn't enjoy it, but his brother knows and is grateful to her for this act of sexual benevolence. Because no one else will have him? Or because in sleeping with Candelario she has indirectly conferred a blessing on the family, the gringa's golden touch. See, it says – in a country where Aryan worship flows undisturbed beneath the surface, where light skin confers higher status, where all things American are good, just and coveted – see? We were chosen. The brother smiles at her all evening. Brings her fresh beer as soon as the one before her is empty. She smiles back, of course, she has been smiling all year as a substitute for the Spanish she still cannot speak, but she is embarrassed by his show of gratitude. The man she slept with is kind but, she discovered last night, a cave man in bed.

She doesn't know how she got into this, Shelley's boy-friend vetoed her first local crush, 'Oh, he's *malo* – bad, you don't want him.' They'd been drinking, Shelley and Dana and Mauricio, in effect a kind of *despedida* atmosphere has been going on for days now. It started as a silly parlour game, drunk talk, Dana rhyming off the names of the men she thought were attractive, Mauricio responding with *si, no* or *tal vez*, maybe, but he was serious and had, she guesses now, his own choice already made. Tonight Dana feels that it is all quite out of her hands, a game with invisible rules that is only half over. Stupid to have said yes to it. Stupid to have let hormones, booze and sincere affection for Mauricio sway her.

Dana suspects that what makes her attractive here is what she represents, a land of perceived plenty and desire, far from the river and the small fishing village. But with Mauricio as Cupid, she has left the territory of dry abstraction, and now she's up to her neck in the swift clear current of machismo. Her friend and 'coach' wave from the shore, cheering her on.

Candelario had been invited last night to the house on stilts that she and Shelley have shared for the past year. Watching him cross the yard, Dana felt a combination of trepidation and disappointment.

He was wearing crisply ironed jeans and a navy golf-shirt. The black loafers on his feet had probably been carried to just within sight of the house, because of the mud and puddles that dotted the road. Out of his beach apparel – old shorts and a bare chest or ripped T-shirt – he'd lost the libidinous appeal that made her offer his name in the first place.

He'd delivered an elaborate monologue as he prepared the *encocada*, fish stewed in coconut juice. Dana had been edgy and distracted before dinner, only in part because she didn't understand what he was saying. But the meal had been exquisite. She'd mimed looks of rapture at the taste and repeated a

few of her stock phrases, '*deliciosa*' and '*que rico*', until someone landed a smart kick to her shin under the table. She
yelped and found Shelley glaring at her, with a look that
demanded, What-is-wrong-with-you?! Nerves, Dana wanted
to reply, because she knew he'd end up staying, knew she had
lost whatever lust she'd felt for him before and from afar.

She could think of no way to boot him out at the end of the
night. Mauricio and Shelley had offered to sleep on the balcony, leaving her the indoor bed, both of them still miraculously oblivious to her mounting panic. And so Candelario
had stayed, and perhaps he too had a case of nerves, or being
the man felt there was something to prove. She almost wished
she'd been the fish, because he'd shown real finesse with that,
and besides she'd be in some kind of piscine heaven, a gilled
and swimming angel instead of sweating it out on these sheets
with a jackhammer.

The sex had been lousy, painful even.

But to put an end to it now requires skills she doesn't have,
a perfect navigation of gender and culture. Somehow, reputa-
tions are involved: Mauricio's, Candelario's, maybe even
Shelley's. What Dana feels or wants to say is the part that
doesn't fit, the part that would be perceived as insult, as
undertow. So, for better or worse – one more night – she's
going 'with the flow'. She allows herself a silent disloyalty,
referring to her new lover as the Neanderthal.

Nicknames abound here, but this isn't one she could share
with anyone but Shelley. Not Gaby, who has troubles enough
in the shape of her bad-boy husband. Dana wouldn't take on a
man like El Capitan for all the money in the world. Handsome but high-maintenance, he's the sort who needs a new
challenge every two months. The latest of these is the beautiful shrimp farm upriver where he's installed Gaby and their
little boy, Tomas.

She looks over to where the Capitan is holding forth in a

corner of the bar, the devoted Gaby at his side, laughing too hard at his jokes. The other men occasionally interject, egging Capi on, patting Gaby on the shoulder at the funny parts.

Dana suspects that capturing a gringa's heart was just another of Capi's projects, something to which he applied his not inconsiderable charm and talent. If it hadn't been for the baby, and Gaby's desperate tenacity, the wedding would never have taken place.

Another squeal of hilarity greets what must be a punch line. Dana wonders if they're keeping the whole town awake. The bar is really just a big porch around two rooms, a *bodega* for storage and minimal cooking, and a smaller room with a cot, where drunks from neighbouring villages sometimes sleep it off. The walls of these, inside and out, have recently been painted a vivid yellow. Tonight the bar is humming with noise, a glowing beacon on a moonless night, overlooking the *boca* or mouth of the Cojimies river where it meets the Pacific. Beyond the small boats that litter the beach just above the tideline, she can only just make out a glimmer of phosphorescence where the water laps at the sand. She can't see the horizon but knows it well, dense mangrove punctuated by towering royal palms. Two miles upriver and accessible through a series of channels is the shrimp farm.

Dana's been there, ostensibly to practise her Spanish. More accurately, she's found herself on the front lines of marital warfare. She's witnessed the various skirmishes, watched Gaby, American-gone-bush, weep dreary tears from the blue eyes that originally won her the Capitan's attentions. Depending on his mood or the time of day, how much he's had to drink and whether or not he's recently been to town, Capi either ignores his wife, teases her or explodes with anger and storms out of the house to his boat waiting below at the river dock. Everyone – except Gaby herself – knows why. He finds reasons to go downriver more and more frequently. Gaby stays behind with Tomas and a cadre of servants, fretting and eating. She's fat now, says Capi likes her that way, something to hold on to that the other men won't want to steal. Dana hears the insult in that. Wonders how her friend manages not to.

Candelario has stationed himself at Dana's table, proprietorial. Obviously she is 'allowed' to dance with all the others tonight, in fact, is expected to, but he is letting the town know where he'll be going at the end of the party. Out of bed, in spite of their limited ability to converse, she likes him. She likes all the men here. As a gringa she's had far more exposure to them than the women. But in general she'd say that if there is such a thing as town character, this place is good and kind and laughs a lot. People call each other *vagos*, meaning lazy, but they're not, any of them would work thirty-six hours straight to help a neighbour repair a damaged roof or redig an exhausted well. Kids in this town crawl up on the closest lap, ensured of an affectionate response.

Candelario already has two children by different women. Guiltily, Dana knows he will love her best and longest because she's going away tomorrow and won't be returning. But for now he is the proud 'partner'; he will come back to the house with her tonight and she is already so sore.

Food keeps appearing miraculously in wide enamel trays. Someone has slaughtered a pig. It is being roasted in a nearby *caña* house by an unseen woman, the wife of one of these happy, drinking men. Dana is embarrassed, feels like a charlatan. All this adulation because she is *la gringa rubia*, the only blond other than fat Gaby. Shelley knows the protocol. 'Eat the meat,' she hisses, although Dana used to be a vegetarian. 'This is a big deal,' Shelley warns, 'eat it.' Dana eats another piece of roasted meat, wants to go home to sleep, wants to avoid another night of clumsy sex. More beers. More dancing. Someone comes to her table bearing an enamel dish of the roasted pork with slices of plantain fried to a golden crisp and hot sauce in a small jar. Dana takes some. Smiles at the charming man carrying the tray, '*Que rico*,' she murmurs, between small bites.

Where's Gaby? The Capitan is dancing up a storm and shouting at everyone. Shelley has had more to drink than Dana but neither of them is as drunk as Gaby when they finally find her lying at the bottom of one of the wooden *canoas* hauled up on the beach. She is crying. Maria Luisa, whose husband supports two other households, has told her about the Capitan's lover. She doesn't dislike the Capitan, she's just fed up with the men who drink her beer and eat her excellent clam *cebiche* on credit. She knows women need to stick together. The village is growing exponentially.

They lead Gaby back to the bar. Her skirt is rumpled and her nose is running. She cracks the Capitan over the head with a beer bottle. There is blood and broken glass in all directions. The *despedida* is over, although traditionally it is meant to go on until dawn. First Gaby is trying to hold a wet cloth to the cut on her husband's brow, sobbing all the while. Now she is demanding a bottle of gentian violet from Maria Luisa. She aims erratically at Capi's forehead with the glass wand but she has drunk too much to do it properly. Purple antiseptic dribbles down his temples and cheeks as he brushes her hand away. Dana suppresses the urge to laugh. The Capitan can't decide what mood to be in. First he is yelling and hopping around in his socks, then he is the maudlin orator, proclaiming his misfortune in all directions, making a further fool of the snuffling Gaby. Shelley and Dana exchange looks. He will be in town tomorrow night with his mistress. The cut on his head is not serious and will bring sympathy from his woman in town, ribald praise from his friends. The young happy men have drifted home to sleep. Candelario is waiting to walk Dana back to Shelley's house on the beach. There is blood on Gaby's blue skirt as Maria Luisa leads her to the spare room at the back of the yellow bar. The Capitan makes a great show of walking down to the water, announcing he will sleep in his boat, he will hang his head over the side, he will bleed into the river and the fish will drink his blood, spilled in the name of love. He has what remains of a bottle of rum in his hand.

Shelley and Dana walk through the night-black town to the house on stilts. The house faces the ocean, a fair distance from the town proper, past the graveyard and the local bordello. They walk with flashlights aimed at the ground ahead to avoid the piles of shit and the holes in the road. To either side of them, fireflies punctuate the dark shadows between coco palms. Some yards behind and conversing in hushed tones walk the two men, Candelario and Mauricio.

Mauricio is Shelley's first Latin boyfriend. She says the sex is so-so but he is a joyful, laughing man and she is learning the nuances of the language. Dana can't imagine that the sex is as bad as it will be for her tonight in the cane house on the foam bed, the whole structure creaking with the sideways thrusts of this fisherman. He must think this is the way Americans make love. He must think this is pleasurable, an homage suitable to *la reina del Cojimies* or 'town queen', the nickname Dana has earned, her blondness a kind of crown. Dana has already tried to restrain him with her muscles, with the pressure of her hands on his back, his hips. She cannot think of the Spanish words to say it. Not like that. You're hurting me. Stop.

The house shakes with his ardor. While Shelley and Mauricio giggle quietly from their mattress on the balcony, the house sways back and forth, its floor reverberating, its cane walls shaking and creaking. Dana is concentrating, not on her own pleasure, impossible under the circumstances, but in moving her body to minimize the discomfort and pain. It's worse of course, she's feeling bruised and tender from the night before. It takes a while for the obvious to occur to her, that he's waiting for a signal and, receiving none, is almost desperately and mechanically 'lasting'. She'd laugh if it didn't hurt so much. She moans and hopes the sounds of pain are masquerading as sexual response. He seems to buy it. Her hands slide on his back at the sudden release of sweat; moments later his own cry signals the end. He collapses onto the bed beside her and then lifts his head to plant one tired kiss on her forehead.

She pats his shoulder. Within minutes he is snoring. They have not exchanged more than a few words all evening. Dana is embarrassed at how little Spanish she has acquired. Sleepily, she runs down the list of reasons. Shelley has been an able translator, Gaby a distracted tutor. But though she's tried, though she's received compliments on her accent, Dana has been a slow student, unable or unwilling to pass through a certain wall.

Now, with her year drawing to a close, regret at remaining on the periphery has spawned this last-minute dive – into what? The community? Cross-cultural fucking, she berates herself, isn't the solution. Dana sighs and shifts onto her side. Behind her, Candelario stirs, clears his throat and cuddles up behind her. He slings a heavy, muscular arm around her ribs, cupping a hand around one breast. Gently, so as not to wake him, she takes his hand away but then doesn't know where to put it. She holds it for a few minutes, their two arms suspended in the air. Well? Finally, sandwiching his calloused hand between her two palms, she brings it up under her chin. He's stopped snoring. The last sound she hears before falling asleep is the wind breathing lightly through the cracks in the cane walls.

In town the next morning, they are loading the boat,

people hurrying up and down the beach and sacks of produce piled at the bottom of the gangplank for transport to a city further south. Two of her dancing partners from the *despedida* wink as they trot past, T-shirts around their heads like turbans, to cushion the stack of plastic *javas* each is carrying down to the boat. There is a rhythmic sound of clinking glass.

Gaby is waiting for them at the water. She has, as they say here, 'dawned crying', nursing a wicked hangover and still smelling of rum as she hugs Dana goodbye. And no one knows where Capi is, a tiny smear of blood on his boat causing Gaby to burst into a fresh spate of tears. Mauricio is teasing everyone. 'The fish ate him!' he says to Gaby who simply cries harder. He's dancing circles around the gringas, winking at Shelley and expressing great sadness at their parting, even though Shelley, he knows, will be returning in a week to the coast.

Candelario has carried Dana's heavy bag all the way from the house to the ship, he stows it on board for her and descends the wooden plank again for a last hug on the beach, begging Dana to come back, not to stay away too long, '*Mi amor, mi carino*', and later as the town recedes and the ship starts to roll with the swell, Dana winces as she sits on her canvas bag, saying to her tall friend, 'Well, Shell, love hurts.' A smile crosses Shelley's face and fades almost instantly. It's her usual seasickness, compounded by the indulgences of last night. An old man in a battered hat sits next to them, the small cut above his eyebrow painted with gentian.

Coming out of the *boca*, they swing to port. Dana watches the beach slide by at a distance, tall palms succeeded by low fences and then more palms and the occasional thatched roof of a fisherman's cottage. She has walked it daily for months but from here it's a toy landscape and this, the diminishing and unfamiliar view, part of a journey back to the country called home.

Already, she misses things, Gaby's fried cheese and Capi's antics, Mauricio's impish grin and even, she realizes with a shock, the feel of Candelario's hand between her hands. Years like this are the stuff of memories, swirling together in the wake of this slow, rolling boat heading south through the Pacific, their colour a mixture of Capi's red blood and Gaby's blue tears or a violet smudge on a wound that won't heal, not life-threatening but persistent. Tender to the touch.

# *A la Playa*

───────

YOU CAN PICTURE this from a bird's-eye view. A pair of heads, two sets of shoulders, his more deeply tanned than yours. The artist in you, storing the image for further use, notes – true to the conventions of Egyptian tomb painting – he/dark, she/light. Four arms like noodles out over the fat shiny tire, bobbing on an immensity of sparkling, swelling green. Beneath the surface, shadowy wiggles, four legs like tentacles drooping from the big black octopus head.

Toes touching his and then sand, drifting toward beach, towards rocks, one foot glancing off, oooo-what-is-it, something weird and woolly. Snaps you back into the tube and out of your airborne vision, dumps your consciousness into the immediate. He grunts. You produce a little shriek.

In a few minutes the two of you will haul it up the beach, an old net in the shape of a body, you'll pull out the coral snagged in the folds, the shells and jagged cups of barnacle, chewed-up cork, hooks, and here and there a knotted mass of line, all of it complicated and compacted into this thing that weighs as much or more than a drowned sailor and the excitement and mystery of it will fade when it proves itself to be nothing more than a drowned net.

After the dip you rinse off in brackish water from the shower head attached to your host's house. The water gouts and sputters and then leers out of a plastic clown face screwed to mouldy cement. Some days you soap up but the ungainly squat and your hand shovelling at the crotch of your suit; the fact that everybody smells the same, of sweat and tanning lotion and bug cream and beer; and sometimes just the weird red grin leering at you from around the shower nozzle, makes you hold back from being too scrupulous in your ablutions. Instead you let the water decide, running down over your head and shoulders. You snap the sleek black tanksuit away from your cleavage, once, twice. You can't really be bothered getting cleaner than this.

The man loves you but you won't fuck. He won't try and you won't invite. You'll share a bed and snuggle a bit, until with a sigh you say, 'Too hot,' and push him away. But you're at the beach, so you think about sex a lot, it's accumulating in layers like the creams and lotions on your skin, like the slightly greasy feel of sea air, another epidermis, laid on and glued down by wind.

You find the toucan head on the first day, walking alone towards Tonchigue, the fishing village a mile south of where you stay. It's strange, a red and yellow and green hook of a thing, hanging just out of reach on a dried stalk, reed-like, part of a parched bush backed up against a cliff. You throw pebbles and shells at it before you know what it is, trying to shake it loose from its perch. Finally you go in search of a stick and flip what you now recognize as a beak over your head. You wonder where the bird died, not here, higher probably; and this, the part the vultures didn't want, was dropped and where it snagged and stuck the only things to find it were the ants that have picked it almost clean. The lower beak hangs slack, bleached, still attached but tenuously, by black cords of sinew or skin. The skull is perfect, smooth on top and at the sides. Only underneath are there scraps of leathery flesh. One round dried marble of an eyeball clicks against the beak. It stinks. You carry it back to the house, wondering what invisible form of lice might now be travelling from dead bird to live woman, setting up shop on sunburnt skin, crawling through the forest of fine blond hairs on a forearm. You perch the skull on the sharpened cane fence of your host's house. It presides over the visit, a bird god. Sightless, silent, beaky.

Later that night you are at the beach-side bar run by the balding Italian with the lisp whose body is firm and muscular, whose balls bulge in a skimpy thong underneath his designer T-shirt. He rescues his pet spider monkey from a clutch of taunting squealing children on the balcony. The monkey is squealing too. The Italian brings it on its string leash to where you are half seated, half splayed out, an awkward position dictated by the mad mechanics of the wooden deck chair into which you melted after too much lobster and too many beers. He introduces the monkey to your lap as if the two might be made for each other, at least the monkey thinks so, and the man, as an afterthought, looks at your face and queries, *'Te molesta?'* Does it bother you?

You have never had a monkey in your lap before and you are wondering what kind of lice or fleas or tics or chiggers are housed in its short sleek fur or alternatively what kind of disease you will contract if it bites you, what about that AIDS theory, the thoughts spin and shuck and drop in your mind like tumblers on Lottario day and you decide, never mind, death by tropical infection or infestation, and you say, *'No, no me moleste,'* because the feel of the monkey in your lap and its delicate fingers on your arm and its dear bleached scalp are worth the thousand terrors that have somersaulted through your consciousness in the last ten seconds. It's like a baby. You want a baby. But on a balmy night beside the ocean, just north of the equator, on a night when no baby has yet appeared, miraculous, in your womb, you discover that a spider monkey, temporarily, will do.

At the beach you hardly ever bathe. You dip in and out of salt water and salt air and accumulate layers. Of fish juice and the cold drips running down beer bottles onto your skirt, bug repellent, sun lotion, the squeeze of lemon over *cebiche*, the shrimp guts and squid ink that paint your palms and fingernails and arms and legs. You are becoming biosphere and the ocean breeze circles you like a testimony, like a story of your new and ancient self.

You always feel like this on the beach, naked and yet not, solid and yet permeable. Usually horny as hell. Wet sand underfoot – you can't get enough walking – you want to walk the coastal length of this continent but you turn back before Tonchigue, you turn back at the pier, iced like a cake with frigates and vultures and pelicans, the memory of its attachment to land hanging still in the emptiness between it and the shore. Dozens of birds. The white throat sacks of the frigates, the yawn and stretch of an occasional pelican shaking its pouch for a snack, the preternatural brood of vultures hulking higher up on the abandoned shed at the end of the pier.

You hardly ever bathe at the beach because there's a metal trunk in the shower stall of the one bathroom and the toilet is lined in grime and salt rime and always smells like someone just took a dump. For the first few days you are not aware of the other bathroom, ensuite to the master bedroom. You have already postulated that your host has adopted the habit of 'doing a growler' – this is the language your friends use – in the ocean. You know most men in this country pee on bushes and hedges and fences and walls and tires or on nothing but the baked brown dirt out behind houses. By the time you discover that this other bathroom exists, with its relatively clean and private tub, you have resigned yourself to the salt and fish stink of your skin. The knowledge of this extra bathroom is a luxury item in the file of your brain. You categorize it under non-necessities.

One day it rains and you stand under it, letting it slick down your body. The man who loves you wants to help you wash. He hasn't seen your breasts in seven years or your bare ass in twelve. You were lovers once, that long ago, and for nostalgia or something less definable you shared a bed the last time you visited this strange and wonderful country, but he was still married and so you kept your panties on and now time has solidified the feelings between you but the motions are more difficult. He pours buckets of rain water over your head. You use shampoo. Your body feels babe-like and rubbery. You say to yourself that you're washing off years. The palm fronds drip all afternoon. The man who loves you makes lazy proposals of marriage that involve varying increments of weight loss for him and waiting for you. All day long, he plans a fish chowder. You help him by looking in a stained and tattered cookbook, whose back cover and several pages are missing. From D onwards the index is gone. You settle for *bouillabaisse*. The flies thicken the soupy air inside the house. Fish heads bubble on the stove. One eyeball floats to the surface, opaque as a cataract. You think of Innu children but can't bring yourself to snack on the proffered delicacy.

You force the man who loves you to 'talk turkey' about his plans. You are relentless, insistent as a dentist's drill. He keeps reaching for *The Joy of Cooking* as a way of changing the subject, an ineffectual detour from the single track you're on, fish soup be damned. You alternate tough questions with your own assessment of his life so far. You cite examples of older expatriate drunks. 'Don't end up like them,' you say. His eyes are hurt behind the Polaroid lenses of his glasses when he responds, 'You think I haven't thought of it?'

The next day you're swinging lazy in the hammock in the red light of late afternoon. He stands over you and, with his thigh, stops you mid-sway. Leaning over the hammock, he says, 'You're in danger of becoming a bitch,' and pauses. Then, taking courage from your silence, he goes on, 'Because you're so opinionated.'

You resist the urge to fight back. He has a point. You could argue his choice of words but not his right to say this from out of the vulnerable part of him you exposed yesterday like a surgeon. You know you are like a drug to him and that he doesn't yet know how much he can take, neither the allowable dosage nor the frequency. He is at sea in you. He is a little boat tossed about on your waves and you are the great devouring saltwater womb. You don't mean to be but that's not the issue. Whatever you do keeps tossing him high in spray-filled air and flinging him down on a drum-hard beach. Bitch.

His body has aged outward, flesh hanging heavy on his medium build. His hair has developed that indeterminate colour exhibited by men in their fifties. He is regrowing the moustache he had for over twenty years that the Ecuadorian girlfriend convinced him to shave off. He is deeply tanned and weathered and uses his body well, which makes the girth of him bearable to you, who are so vain about appearances. You tease him about his gut. His toes and ankles are those of a fisherman, gnarled and choked with varicose veins. A great scar like a sickle embraces him under his ribs, a chunk of liver gone, delivered finally onto an operating table after years of recurrent malaria made worse by drink.

He's done his share of drugs too. Cocaine for the most part. He's separated from the wife who has not stopped huddling over the smoking screen, who is enticed back *ad nauseam* to the sweet sickly stink of base and all that it fitfully promises. He thinks of you as the love of his life but you know you've only earned the title by default. The part of you that isn't a bitch worries that you've pared him down too much, too close to the bone. But instead you say, 'I was worried that I was just a symbol to you.' This, after his prediction of your impending status as the kind of woman men avoid. He is stunned. Hurt.

'Symbol of what?'

You don't say it but you think it – the light princess. Sunshine, laughter. All that she isn't, now. Snow White or Cinderella compared to his wife, a burnt-out Dragon Queen. You remember just in time that everyone is human. Even you. He has treated you with gentle humour and affection all week. You wonder what it is about softness in a man that brings out the talons in you and at the same time this icy shield. You love him too, in a way that you can never admit, because the pity part of it may be for something in yourself. That after all these years, this is the marriage you are offered, the pairing, perhaps, that you deserve.

You acquiesce enough each night to kiss him good night before you turn to sleep on your side at the edge of the bed facing the door. Knowing that in your dreams, you'll veer towards the symbolic, wanting to be sure of an escape route. You poke him when he snores. He does, with regularity. In the morning you ask if you snored too. 'Gently,' he says, 'I could hardly hear it.' He goes on, 'It's sweet.' And more, 'Kinda sexy.' You have to admit you love the way he loves you. No demands. You don't know if you could have sex with him any more. A rhetorical question. It strikes you that it would be easy to marry him. That maybe sex leaves so many marriages because it's the volatile component, the need and heat. You can imagine yourself growing old with him, trading off more and more of the gender roles. He loves to cook and doesn't mind cleaning. You tell him he'll have to teach you how to take apart the engine of his Harley. You like this man. He is as calm as a rock, as rooted as a tree and only windblown where you're concerned. You love the way he treats you, moving around your perimeter with gentle wariness, with solid affection. When he takes you to the bus in Esmeraldas, the one that will take you away from him, he reaches for your hand as you cross the street.

Holding hands with him is the most comfortable place you've been in eight years. You do not tell him this. You board the bus after wriggling out of his sweaty grasp. You are going to miss him like mad.

You wash the beach off you as soon as you arrive back in the city. You stand for half an hour under hot water. You knead your scalp and suds your armpits, you scrub at the unrealized potential of him between your legs. You wash it all away, the need, the possibility, the kindness of him, the sweaty fish-stinkiness of sea. You rinse clear of the past and the future. Sand swirls in the tub and down the drain. You step out.

## Acknowledgements

'Orchids' first appeared in *Grain*, Winter 1996 and 'A La Playa' in *PRISM international*, Winter 1996.

'Orchids', 'Nickname' and 'A La Playa' appeared in *Coming Attractions 96* published by Oberon.

'Hatchetface' will appear in *The Summit Anthology*, forthcoming from The Banff Centre Press.

Kelley Aitken has been published in a number of literary journals and anthologies. She is a painter, a teacher and a freelance illustrator in Toronto.